ANIMAL
ALERT
HEATWAVE

Animal Alert series

ANIMAL
ALERT

HEATWAVE

Jenny Oldfield

*Hodder
Children's
Books*

a division of Hodder Headline plc

Special thanks to Julie Briggs of the RSPCA. Thanks also to
David Brown and Margaret Marks of Leeds RSPCA Animal
Home and Clinic, and to Raj Duggal MVSc, MRCVS and Louise
Kinvig BVM & S, MRCVS

First published in Great Britain in 1999
by Hodder Children's Books

British Library Cataloguing in Publication Data
A Catalogue record for this book is available from the
British Library

ISBN 0 340 74682 3

Typeset by Avon Dataset Ltd, Bidford-on-Avon, Warks
Printed and bound in Great Britain by
The Guernsey Press Co. Ltd, Channel Isles

Hodder Children's Books
a division of Hodder Headline plc
338 Euston Road
London NW1 3BH

1

'*How many cats?*' Paul Grey tapped his pen on the desk as he spoke into the phone. He nodded at Carly for her to open the doors for the start of morning surgery.

'It's hot!' she muttered to herself. The sun blazed down on the carpark. Windscreens glinted, the smell of melting tar hit her. 'Hot, hot, hot!'

'. . . *Twelve!*' Paul received an answer to his question and sounded surprised. 'Are you sure? You're telling me that there are twelve feral cats living wild on King Edward's Road allotments?'

'Hi, Carly. You look hot!' Liz Hutchins, the junior

vet at Beech Hill, breezed in through the main doors carrying a cardboard box. 'Hedgehog!' she explained briskly. 'Found in my neighbour's back garden.'

'What's wrong with it?' Carly followed Liz back across the waiting area. Behind them, a trickle of patients slowly filed in.

'His leg's trapped inside a metal ring-pull from a drinks can. See.' Slipping on a pair of thick gloves from behind the reception desk, Liz lifted a prickly, speckled ball from the box. The little hedgehog's head and three legs were tucked out of sight, but the fourth leg trailed limply.

Carly frowned at the aluminium ring. It was squashed out of shape, cutting into the hedgehog's upper leg. A patch of dried blood showed that it had been there for some time. 'I'll fetch some clippers to cut through the metal,' she offered.

'Thanks. I'll take him into Room Two.' The young vet put the hedgehog back into the box.

'. . . If you want us to run a welfare check on twelve cats, we need permission from the council to go on their property to bring them in.' Paul glanced at his watch. 'Listen, Steve, I'll talk to you when you get back, OK?'

2

'. . . Melanie!' Carly went looking for their nurse to ask for clippers. She ran down the corridor to the kennels, to be greeted by a barrage of loud barks and whines from the dogs. No sign there of the nurse, so she backed out and skipped upstairs to look in the cattery.

'You'll find clippers in the prep room!' Paul called up after her. He'd put down the phone and was checking his list of appointments.

So, downstairs again, almost bumping into her dad's first patient: a limping, grey cross-breed dog and her young owner. 'Sorry!' Carly muttered. *Hot!* she thought, pushing her dark hair from her face. *Sweaty, sticky hot*.

The clean white surfaces of the prep room gleamed; the white-tiled walls reflected the light. Choosing strong clippers from a steel tray, Carly hurried back to Liz and the hedgehog.

'. . . Hi there, Lucy.' Paul pulled on his white coat and held open the door of Treatment Room 1 for the limping dog and her blonde owner. 'So what's Suzi been up to?'

The dog hobbled in on her sore paw; the door closed.

Carly dashed on.

'Carly!' Bupinda, the receptionist, appeared in the office doorway. She nodded towards the double glass doors of the main entrance, to where Carly's friend, Hoody, stood with his dog, Vinny.

'Not now!' Carly mouthed the words at him, guessing that he wanted her to fetch a dog from the kennels and walk with him and Vinny in the park. 'Too busy!'

But, dressed in a shapeless grey-white T-shirt and worn out jeans, Hoody refused to shift. He held up what looked like an empty milk bottle.

'What?'

He pointed at the bottle.

'What?' Carly said again. She gestured impatiently for Hoody to come inside. Nipping into Room 2 to drop off the cutters for Liz, she dashed out again. *Boiling. Baking. Melting in the heat.*

'Mouse.' Hoody had left Vinny on the step and come into the waiting room. He scowled at her, bottle held up for her to see.

In the bottom of the grimy bottle, a small grey creature scrabbled.

Carly gasped and went closer. 'How . . . ?'

'Dunno.' Hoody cut her short. 'Just found it in the alley at the back of Hillman's.'

'It must have been able to squeeze in, but now it can't get out. It's trapped!' She peered at the mouse inside the bottle. Its little claws scratched and slipped on the smooth glass as it reached up on its hind legs.

'Yeah.' Hoody handed it over to Carly. 'What was I supposed to do? I couldn't just leave it, could I?'

'No . . . thanks!' Taking charge, Carly tilted the bottle gently. She gave the mouse a chance to scuttle along its length. But when it came to the neck and tried to squeeze its head and shoulders through, she saw that it panicked in the narrow gap and retreated.

'Your dad will know what to do.' Sticking his hands in his pockets, Hoody turned away. 'Vinny and me are off to the park,' he told her.

'Yeah, see you!' Absent-mindedly, Carly sighed then carried the trapped mouse towards the desk.

'Poor Hoody!' Bupinda murmured, phone cradled under her chin, staring at the boy's back view as he left the building.

'Why "Poor Hoody"?' *Poor mouse*! was what Carly was thinking.

'In case you hadn't noticed he was asking you if

you wanted to go to the park with him and you knocked him back.' The kind receptionist spoke up for the shabby, tough-looking kid who was walking, shoulders hunched, across the carpark.

'He'll live,' Carly replied. Not that she didn't care about hurting Hoody's feelings; they were good friends and she wanted to keep it that way. But she was baking in the midday heat, she was busy and she was exhausted.

Gently she put the bottle on the desk and watched the mouse struggle to escape. Its claws rattled against the glass, its whiskers and ears twitched, it squeaked and pleaded to be let out.

'Soon!' Carly promised the mouse that it would be the next patient to be seen.

Then – after the mouse – Mr Waring with his cat, Tibs; then the boy with the parrot in the cage; then a woman called Vivian and her cocker spaniel, Bonnie . . .

A hedgehog injured by a drinks can, twelve wild cats to be brought in, a mouse in a bottle – except for the blinding, never-ending heat of this freak August weather, for Carly this was just another ordinary day at Beech Hill Rescue Centre.

* * *

'Have a shower,' Paul suggested, studying his hot and bothered daughter at the end of morning surgery. Melanie, Bupinda and Liz had already gone on their lunch break. Only he and Carly were left in the building. 'Or go to the baths, have a quick swim.'

The hedgehog's leg had been cleaned up, the mouse was free from the bottle. Carly had wiped down the tables in the treatment rooms and mopped the floors. A dip in cool, clear water sounded great, but she was feeling guilty about Hoody. 'I think I'd better take a dog to the park,' she sighed, thinking he and Vinny might still be there.

'How about the German shepherd?' Her dad suggested one of the rescue dogs who was proving hard to re-home. Rusty was a handful: big, strong and easily bored. Any new owner would have to provide him with lots of space and exercise.

But before Carly had time to organise an outing, Steve Winter's van screeched into the carpark and pulled up at the door. One glance at the inspector's face as he jumped out and flung open the back doors told them that they had an emergency on their hands.

'Stand by!' Paul warned, striding to meet Steve. 'What have you got?'

'Heatstroke victim.' The inspector hurried into the building carrying a limp black-and-white dog: a short-haired terrier type whose tongue lolled out of his open mouth. His head was hanging, his eyes closed. 'Left in a car in the supermarket carpark,' Steve explained. 'No windows open, no shade. It was like an oven in there!'

'Idiot owner!' Carly's dad delivered a stern verdict, one eye on a second car pulling up outside. An anxious, shame-faced man in a blue, open-necked shirt got out. 'Don't people ever learn?'

'How bad is he?' Carly held open the prep room door for Steve and the patient.

'Unconscious. Rapid pulse. Dehydrated.' The inspector laid the dog on a table and stood back to let Paul take over. 'A few more minutes inside that metal box and he'd have had it. Luckily, a passer-by spotted him and flagged down my van.'

Carly watched anxiously as her father used his stethoscope to listen for a heartbeat. The little dog lay motionless under the bright light.

'Right, we need to set up a drip!' Paul decided.

So Carly wheeled a metal stand close to the table, while her father rigged up the saline solution that would save the dog's life. She watched the needle go in under the skin, and handed him some tape to strap it into position. Within seconds, the drip was working.

Paul stood back, ready to go and tackle the patient's owner. 'Let's hope there's no permanent damage,' he muttered, stripping off his surgical gloves and ditching them in the disposal unit. He swung out through the prep room door.

'. . . Your dog lost a lot of body fluid,' he was explaining calmly as Steve and Carly followed him out. 'We hope we got to him in time, but it's a case of wait and see.'

'I only left him for five minutes!' the man in the blue shirt protested. 'I had to dash and pick up a prescription from the chemist. When I came back, I found your inspector guy breaking the back window!'

Carly allowed herself a quick glance at the owner. A short, fat, balding man with a shiny forehead, his palms were spread upwards as he proclaimed his innocence. She frowned at Steve. No way would she have been as polite and patient with him as her dad was trying to be. There was a dog lying close to death in the room next door, all because of this man's carelessness and ignorance.

'Come on.' Steve called Carly over to the desk. 'Help me fix up a visit to the allotments to pick up these feral cats.'

Glad to change the subject while her dad reassured the man and showed him to the door, she went to the phone book to find the council number. 'What happens when we bring the cats in?' she asked.

'First off, we check to see that none are sick or injured. After we've vaccinated them, we separate off the ones that aren't totally wild.'

'Do we try to find homes for them?'

Steve nodded. He'd rung the department, but was having trouble getting through. 'The ones that are too wild for re-homing have to be put back in the colony. But first we have to neuter them so the feral population doesn't get out of control. Then we tip them.'

Carly's face took on a puzzled frown. 'Meaning?'

'We clip off the very tip of the left ear. It's an identification mark to show that they've been neutered.' Giving up on the number for the time being, Steve put down the phone. 'Did you know, there's probably over one million feral cats in the UK?'

'Wow, no!' The moment Steve put down the phone, it started to ring, so Carly grabbed it. Her walk in the park with Rusty seemed to be getting further away by the second. 'Hello, Beech Hill Rescue Centre!'

'Hello?' A quavery voice spoke, then hesitated.

'Yes?' Carly watched Steve head back into the prep room as her dad carried on talking to an over-excited Mr Blue-shirt outside the main door.

'Is that the animal rescue place?' It was an old woman's voice; posh and dithery.

'Yes. Can I help?'

'Well, I'm not absolutely certain that I'm doing the right thing. I found your telephone number on the noticeboard at Holybridge Bird Sanctuary.'

'Yes.' Carly did her best to be patient. She knew Holybridge; it was across the city to the north, a place where she went with Steve when an injured duck or Canada goose had been brought into Beech Hill. The sanctuary offered a safe temporary home for the bird to recover and be released back into the wild.

'I don't like to interfere, only, I do think on this occasion something should be done,' the old lady continued. 'I mean to say, it's definitely a case of cruelty!'

'What is?' Carly looked at the clock. One-thirty. Her stomach rumbled and she was still melting in the heat.

'What's happening to these poor animals. It's this heatwave; the stream has dried up because we've had no rain for weeks. And now they have no running water to drink.'

'Who's "they", please?' Carly picked up a pen, ready to scribble down information.

'The horses at Greenacres, of course!' The woman on the end of the phone seemed to think that Carly was being slow on the uptake.

'How many horses?' 'Greenacres'; she jotted the name on Bupinda's pad.

'Three. And one's only a baby. I wouldn't normally make a fuss, but I know for a fact that the house has been shut up for the whole of August.'

Carly pieced together a picture. 'So there are two adult horses plus a foal . . . in a field?'

'Yes. In a paddock behind the house. I can see them from my bedroom window.'

'And no one seems to be looking after them?' Alarm bells were ringing inside Carly's head. No fresh water! Horses needed plenty to drink, she knew. She moved on quickly to her next question. 'Could you give me your name and address, please?'

There was a sharp, nervous gasp. 'Oh, really, no, I'd rather not say!'

'OK, where's Greenacres then?' Carly waited a long time for a reply. 'Hello?'

'It's just outside Holybridge, on the North Wootton Road. But perhaps I'm doing the wrong thing!' The old lady's voice grew fainter, even more hesitant than before. 'If anyone were to find out that I'd been interfering . . . I live alone, you see.'

North Wootton Road, Carly wrote quickly, *Outside Holybridge*. 'What's the house number, please? . . . Hello? . . . Are you still there?'

Click. The line went dead.

'Problem?' Paul asked as he came back into reception. He'd noticed the frown lines between Carly's dark eyebrows, the alarm in her brown eyes.

She nodded. 'Three horses in a field without water. No one looking after them.' A heatwave, temperatures soaring into the eighties, no rain forecast. This was serious.

'Whereabouts?' Her dad tuned in straight away.

'That's the problem. Somewhere near Holybridge,

but I couldn't get a full address.'

Peering at her scribbled notes, then screwing his tanned, grey-eyed face into a frown to match his daughter's, Paul Grey made an instant decision. 'Greenacres, North Wootton Road. That's good enough.' He grabbed his keys from the hook and his first-aid bag from under the desk. 'Steve, hold the fort here until Liz gets back. Come on, Carly, let's go!'

2

The city centre sweltered in the heat. The sun had baked the flower beds to dry dust and the patches of grass to faded brown stubble. Haze shimmered from the road surface and fumes from cars hung heavy in the still air.

'What's the hold-up?' Paul wondered, trying to see ahead.

Their queue of traffic had ground to a halt in a concrete underpass, but Carly was relieved that at least they were in the shade. She leaned out of the window for a better view. 'Looks like a car's broken down on the next roundabout.' She could see a police patrol car and an officer re-directing the traffic. As they crawled along, from shade back into bright sunlight, she noticed an old silver estate car, bonnet up, steam hissing from the radiator. 'This is all we need!'

'Keep cool!' Her dad hummed to the radio and scanned the giant billboards lining the street. He grinned. 'OK, so keeping cool wasn't exactly a good choice of phrase on a day like today!'

The whole world seemed choked by exhaust fumes and the smell of hot metal. It scrambled Carly's brain and made her eyes prick and ache. 'Just like Nairobi!' she groaned, thinking about the city in Kenya where she'd been born and where her father had worked when she was a little kid. Carly could just remember it.

Nairobi was where she'd lived when her mum had been alive. Hot sun, dusty streets, ancient buses crammed with workers travelling in from the shanty towns. Nighttime, and cool, clear African skies. A million stars. Stuck in a city traffic jam in a heatwave on a busy Tuesday in August, the sky was what Carly remembered best.

'That's better!' Paul edged past the broken-down car and eased into the stream of traffic taking the motorway route out of town. They gathered speed and passed under the giant blue signs, along an overpass with a brewery to one side, tall tower blocks to the other. Then, after a couple of miles of housing estate, they turned off along a sliproad signed Holybridge.

'What do we do if we find these horses are in as bad a way as the woman said?' Carly asked. It was one thing being called out to dogs locked up and abandoned in flats, or to cats whose owners had gone on holiday and left them without food. But horses were different. They were bigger for a start. 'We can't just stick them in Steve's van and take them back to Beech Hill, can we?'

'True.' Paul checked his mirror and signalled right. Turning off, they followed a road surrounded on either side by big pebble-dashed houses, double-garages and neat front gardens. 'But let's not jump ahead of ourselves. Let's find them first, then decide what needs to be done.'

'Left!' Carly said suddenly. She'd seen a sign to the bird sanctuary

Her dad reacted quickly, taking the turning she'd

indicated. Soon there were fields, small patches of woodland and large houses dotting the hillsides on either side. 'OK, now once we reach Holybridge, we need the North Wootton Road.'

Carly kept her eyes peeled. After another mile, a pub and a petrol station told her that they'd passed through the village. She recognised the stone pillars at the entrance to the Holybridge bird sanctuary; its painted sign and winding driveway, the manmade lake in grounds that had once belonged to a grand estate. The house had been pulled down long ago, and the land turned into a haven for birds.

'We must be nearly there!' she muttered. The woman on the phone had mentioned seeing the Beech Hill phone number at the sanctuary, and her voice had sounded like it might belong to one of these big white houses nestling in the trees. Upper class, like them. Not a city voice.

Her dad confirmed that they were on the North Wootton Road. 'These houses are spaced pretty far apart,' he said. 'Most of them don't have numbers; just names.'

Names like Oaktree Cottage and Red Gables, The Old Vicarage and Dower House. Carly scanned them eagerly, then spotted a piebald pony over a hawthorn hedge. 'Stop!' she yelled.

Paul braked and pulled on to the grass verge, while Carly jumped out for a closer look over a wooden gate. The pony trotted up to her in a friendly way. He was sturdy and well groomed and, more importantly, alone in the field.

'No good,' she reported back. 'Are we sure this is the right road?'

'We're not sure of anything.' Her dad signalled and pulled back on to the road. His brow puckered, as if he'd just realised something. 'Remember that place called Dower House?'

'The one with roses growing up it?' She nodded. Surrounded by a tall wall, with its roof of uneven red tiles, it had looked sleepy and old-fashioned. 'Why?'

'There was a lane running down the side of it. I'm just wondering where that might lead.'

Quickly reversing, Paul reached the quaint old redbrick house. They saw that the lane ran between trees which arched overhead. Beyond the trees, tucked out of sight of the main road, there was a more modern house.

'Let's try!' Carly decided.

So they drove slowly down the lane, under the arch of beech trees, round the bend until they came to the closed, double iron gates of the big house.

' "Greenacres"!' Carly and Paul read the name together; white letters on a black sign. The house was set back along a curved drive, built partly of brick, partly of white pebble-dash, with pointed gables decorated with mock Tudor beams. There was a yard and neat outbuildings, and beyond the house more private land.

'Well?' Paul had got out of the car and was staring through the locked gates.

'There's a public footpath down the side here.' Carly walked on and discovered a wooden signpost and a stile leading to a path overgrown with brambles and tall grass. Without waiting for her dad, she climbed the stile and picked her way through the thorny bushes.

'Ouch!' A tendril caught her bare ankle. The thorns had drawn blood. But she was making progress, coming alongside the house. Looking to her left, she could see a field with a white fence, sloping away to trees in a shallow valley. The grass was overgrown with teasels and tall, bright yellow weeds, the surface rough, the grass poor.

'Anything?' Paul yelled from the stile.

She looked again through the shimmering heat and saw the horses. There was a grey on the brow of the hill, standing quite still. The light played tricks and made it look as if he was a wavery mirage: dappled, misty. His head hung low, he sagged. Even when he saw Carly, he didn't move.

'Yes!' she yelled back. Her gaze moved on from the grey horse to a chestnut mare walking slowly into sight. She was thin, her movements heavy and listless, surrounded by a black cloud of buzzing flies. 'Two horses . . . no, three!' she reported, her heart jolting at the sight of the third pathetic creature in the overgrown field.

The foal staggered into view after her mother, the chestnut mare. She was skin and bone. Carly could see each rib in her skinny sides, her legs were like sticks. She walked unsteadily as she struggled to keep up. Deep brown like her mother, her spiky mane and tail were black. The eyes in her large head were dark and dull.

'Dad, come quick!' She realised in a flash that the old lady on the phone hadn't exaggerated the plight of the three horses. They were exhausted and starving, covered in sores, their manes tangled. In fact, far from overstating the truth, she was afraid that the phone call might have come too late.

Paul struggled through the brambles with his first-aid bag. He only needed to take one look before he was over the fence and into the field, heading for the grey horse, whose head sank lower and turned indifferently from him as he approached.

'Easy!' Carly's father reached the horse and took in his terrible condition: the dry, staring coat, the patches of dark sweat. From the tip of his dusty ears to the split and overgrown hooves of his unshod feet, the poor creature cried out neglect.

'What's wrong with him?' Carly knew that the horse's lack of reaction was unnatural. Here was an animal who had gone beyond the impulse to flee from strangers or to put up a fight when they came near. Dazed and lethargic, he breathed and stood with difficulty.

'He's probably dehydrated, like the dog we saw earlier today.' Paul moved in to feel under the horse's cheek for a pulse. Then he ran a hand along his side, leaned in and listened. 'He could have enteritis too, which is an inflammation of the gut.' Glancing at the tall yellow weeds which grew everywhere, he spotted the probable cause. 'That's ragwort,' he told Carly. 'Poisonous to horses. The first thing we have to do is get all three out of here!'

'We need ropes to lead them!' She thought ahead, looked all round the field then up at the house. 'I'll try those outbuildings to see what I can find!'

'Fine. I'll give him a couple of shots; a sedative and an antibiotic.' Her dad opened his bag and got to work, aware that the other two horses also needed his attention. 'Be as quick as you can, and keep out of trouble, OK?'

Carly nodded and began to sprint towards the house, raising cabbage-white butterflies which fluttered away into the blue sky. *Ropes*! she told herself. *Better still, three headcollars to lead the horses to safety*. Beads of sweat stood out on her forehead as she reached the outbuildings to the side of the house.

Stables! Recognising the row of split doors, painted white with neat black hinges, she made up her mind to investigate. Would the bolt in the nearest door slide back? Yes. The top section swung open, and inside the cool, shady room was another door leading to an inner room.

23

Quickly Carly glanced round at the house. Her father had warned her to keep out of trouble. Suppose someone was at home and watching her poke around? They could ring the police and have her thrown off for trespassing. She grew hotter still at the idea, picturing eyes staring at her from behind the curtains in an upstairs window. But then she remembered the three horses. Trespassing or not, she and her dad had to help the poor, neglected creatures.

So she stepped into the stable and tugged at the inner door. It wouldn't open. For a second she thought it must be locked. Then she spotted a loop of blue string roughly knotted to keep the door in place. All fingers and thumbs, she untied it and once more was able to carry on with her search.

The inner room was dark. It smelt stale. Lined with plastic bins and tubs, it was obviously a store place. A couple of faded silk rosettes were pinned to the wall, then further along, as her eyes got used to the gloom, Carly spotted exactly what she was looking for: a row of hooks with ropes and headcollars hanging from them.

She seized them and was outside in a flash, running back to the field, trailing the ropes after her as she climbed the fence. Keeping their distance, the chestnut mare and her foal watched warily.

'How is he?' Carly gasped, reaching her father as he inspected a patch of sore skin on the grey horse's flank. The skin had worn through, the wound had granulated and an infection had set in; in short, it looked a mess.

'He's covered in old saddle sores, weak from thirst, suffering from bowel inflammation . . .' Paul sighed then summed up the horse's prospects. 'I'd rate his chances at no better than fifty-fifty,' he confessed.

'So what do we do?' Slipping a headcollar over his nose and buckling it in place, she clipped a rope to the harness and waited for instructions.

'Is there a place where we can take him out of the sun?' Paul asked.

Carly told him about the row of empty stables.

'What about water?'

'A tap in the yard!' She remembered seeing one as she ran back with the ropes.

'Good, let's go.' Paul took hold of the grey horse's rope and began to lead him gently towards the house. 'You wouldn't believe this to look at him now,' he muttered as they made agonisingly slow progress up the slope, followed from their safe distance by the mare and foal. 'But I'd say this horse has some good breeding behind him. I wouldn't be surprised if he turns out to be pure thoroughbred.'

Carly sighed. She could see what her dad meant; the horse's head was noble, his neck long and graceful. He could be a fine horse – if you ignored the scabs and sores, the dull, sweating coat, the look of misery in his eyes. 'So why let him get into this state?'

'That's what we've got to discover.' Reaching the gate into the yard, Paul waited for Carly to open it. 'Or at least, that'll be Steve's job. But not until after we've sorted all three of them out. I think we get this chap inside and give him an antispasmodic drug to ease the gut problem. Then we set him up with a drip.'

'Why don't we just give him something to drink?' Carly had been right about the tap. It was round the corner from the end stable, dripping and splashing on to the concrete yard.

'He's too far gone. If we made him drink, he'd most likely develop colic. His pulse rate would shoot up even further and I'm pretty sure we'd lose him.' Telling her to go back to the field for the mare and foal, Paul carried out his plan of taking the sick grey horse inside and setting up the drip.

Carly found the chestnut horse standing by the gate, her bay foal at her side. She could tell that though they were nowhere near as bad as the big grey, they too were suffering from the heat. Dazed and confused, they both let her slip on the headcollars and walked across the yard without a murmur. She led them into the stable next door to the grey, closed the door and went to see how her dad was getting on.

He was kneeling over the horse, who lay on his side on a bed of straw. 'Too weak to stand,' Paul explained, his voice tense. 'I've got the drip going, but I need to get back to Beech Hill for more saline solution.'

'I'll stay here!' Carly offered.

Paul thought hard. 'OK. Make sure he doesn't disconnect the drip, keep him nice and quiet. If you can find a rug in any of these stables, lay it over him.'

'What about the other two? Can I give them something to drink?'

Her dad stepped next door to assess the patients. 'Wait for them to cool down, then give the mare a little,' he advised. 'She's still suckling the foal, so she can take her fluid from her mother. Same thing; keep them quiet.'

'And what if someone comes?' As Carly followed Paul into the yard, she glanced up at the silent house.

'Didn't your caller say that the place was shut up?' He followed her gaze, checking the blank windows for signs of life. 'I'll knock on the door on my way out, OK?' Setting off as he spoke, his voice grew fainter. 'If I don't get a reply, we assume that the owners are definitely away.'

Nodding, Carly turned her attention back towards the sick horses. The grey horse lay on his side, breathing unevenly, eyes half closed. She clenched her fists. *How could anyone . . . ?* But there was no point in even finishing the sentence. People did mistreat animals, and that was all there was to it.

A heatwave. An empty house and a mystery caller. And now a battle to treat three parched horses.

Turning on the tap in the yard, Carly made a silent resolution. *We'll do our best*, she promised as cold water splashed her arms and wrists. She cupped both hands and took water to her scorching face. *We'll do all we can to look after you until your owners show up. After that; who knows!*

3

How could you tell if a horse was unconscious or simply sleeping peacefully? Carly wasn't sure. She'd given the mare a small drink from a bucket she'd found in the yard, then left her and her foal settled into the bed of straw that she'd made from an unopened bale in the corner of their stable. Then she'd gone next door to check on the grey. He was lying on his side, legs straight, eyes closed.

For a second she thought he was dead. Then she saw his ribs rise and fall; a shallow, scarcely perceptible movement, but at least he was alive.

Unconscious or sleeping? That was the question.

Carly had been around animals all her life. Every day, injured dogs and cats were brought into Beech Hill. She'd got used to the sight of blood and knew the amazing things that could be done to mend broken bones, sew wide gashes, or cure killer diseases. What's more, she wasn't frightened of any cat or dog. But horses were different, she told herself.

Look at the size of his head, for a start. Carly inched forward into the stable. She gazed down at the pointed ears, the broad brow of the grey horse. His nose was long and straight, his muzzle white and soft, his great nostrils quivering and breathing out warm air. And there was so much muscle in his neck and shoulders. His huge hooves, though split and cracked with neglect, still looked lethal.

Warily she crouched by his head. The eyelids flickered and the blood vessels in his jaw stood out. Under the chin, in the angle between the head and neck, was the spot where you felt for a horse's pulse. She'd watched her dad do it in the field, so she tried it now. If it was fast and uneven, it would mean that the horse's heart was under strain. But no; her fingertips searched for and found a slow, steady beat.

'Just sleeping!' Carly murmured, breathing a sigh of relief. The drip was in place, feeding fluid back into the horse's dehydrated body. Her dad would soon bring more. By evening they might even have him back on his feet.

So she sat in the cool shade of the stable, waiting for her father to return.

The horse breathed steadily. The blinding sunlight visible through the cracks in the door made specks of dust dance and float before her eyes. They began to cast a drowsy spell. Far off, it seemed, an occasional car would drive past, a woodpigeon would coo and call. Sitting in the corner of the dark stable, her knees drawn up to her chin, Carly's eyelids drooped.

Click! Faintly, some way off, a metal latch rose and fell.

Carly jumped. The grey horse's eyes flicked open.

Light footsteps walked across the yard, hesitated, came on.

Like a thief, like a criminal caught in the act, Carly chose to hide. She eased open the inner door leading to the store room and crouched down among the plastic bins.

Waiting while the footsteps drew near, she held her

breath and prayed that she wouldn't be found.

Next door, the mare and foal stirred in their straw. There was a nervous whinny, a stamping of feet. The steps continued, came nearer, then daylight flooded in.

Raising his head, the sick grey horse tried to struggle to his feet. The tube feeding saline solution from the plastic sachet pulled taut. In another moment, the needle might dislodge from under the skin.

'Who is it?' Carly stood up, heart pounding, eyes dazzled by the sudden flood of light. She put up her hand to shade her face.

'Goodness!' a high, cracked voice cried. A figure not much bigger than a child's stood in the doorway. 'You gave me such a fright!'

'Olivia and Kingsley Martyn are in Greece,' the old lady said, five minutes after her sudden appearance. 'That's all I know!'

Carly had recognised the voice of their mystery informant at once.

'. . . Goodness! You gave me such a fright!' Light and refined, like the old ladies who played spinster aunts on TV, she'd shaken and trembled in the doorway as Carly had stepped out of the shadows, one skinny, wrinkled hand to her cheek, the other clutching the frilled neck of her white blouse.

Carly had rushed to explain who she was and what she was doing there. All the while, the grey horse strained and struggled to stand. 'You live next door?' she'd asked the old lady, calming the horse by stroking his neck.

'At Dower House,' she'd confirmed. 'I saw your car leave, so I didn't expect anyone to be here. That's why I had such a fright!'

'Me too!' Carly's heart had only just started to beat normally again. She'd reassured the old lady that the horses were being taken care of and thanked her for calling the rescue centre. Then she'd asked about the horses' owners.

'They're in Greece!' The old lady held back from passing an opinion, but her expression was disapproving.

'For how long? When did they go? Do you know when they're coming back?' Carly came out into the open and buried the neighbour under an avalanche of questions.

'I don't know anything except what I've already told you. The Martyns keep themselves to themselves. But I expect them to be away for the whole of August, as usual.'

'And they left their horses all that time without anyone to look after them? How could they?'

Pursing her thin lips, the old lady considered how the situation must appear, then made an effort to be fair about her neighbours. 'Of course, they couldn't have known that the weather would be so hot and that the stream would dry up . . . and they probably expected Joel to call in and keep an eye on the three horses.'

'Who's Joel?' Carly jumped in with another hasty question.

'Olivia and Kingsley's grown-up son. He's moved out of Greenacres to live in the city centre. I don't like to gossip, but I gather relationships are rather strained. They have a daughter too, of course; Claire. Claire was a sweet girl. She really loved Scottie and Holly.'

'And where is she now?' Carly picked up the old lady's switch to the past tense, and the sad shake of her head.

She pursed her lips tight again. 'I'm afraid I really have no idea.'

Carly realised that this was as far as she was going to get with the polite old lady on the Martyn family background. She made a mental note of the parents' names – Olivia and Kingsley, with unreliable son, Joel, and mysteriously missing daughter, Claire. She would still try for more information about the horses, though. 'Is Scottie this grey horse?'

'Yes. Holly is the chestnut. I don't know the name of her foal, unfortunately.'

Meg! Carly thought up a name on the spot. Nutmeg brown was the colour of her coat. Shortened to Meg, it suited her. 'Thank you, Mrs . . . ?' She was genuinely grateful to the Martyns' shy neighbour. And now she could hear a car turning into the lane and guessed that it must be her dad coming back with extra drugs and fluids for the patients.

'. . . *Miss* Jennings.' The old lady stressed the first word. She too had heard the vet's car arrive and began to make her way across the yard towards the side gate which she'd obviously used to gain entrance. 'You won't mention my part in all this when the Martyns return, will you?' Flustered and fluttery at the idea of being drawn into any unpleasantness, she paused to plead with Carly.

Carly was delivering her promise when the gate burst open and Hoody appeared. The sun beat down on his scowling white face and stubble haircut. Every stain on his T-shirt, every rip in his faded jeans showed up in the glare of the afternoon rays.

'Goodness!' Miss Jennings took two steps back.

Next Vinny bounded into the yard; black and brown, barrel-shaped body bursting with energy, thin tail wagging. He whipped past the hem of the old lady's pleated skirt, making a beeline for Carly.

'It's OK. This is my friend, Hoody,' Carly explained to the Martyns' frightened neighbour. She didn't blame Miss Jennings for thinking he might be some back-street thug. 'Wipe that scowl off your face!' she hissed at him, dragging him forward to be introduced. Then, still under her breath, as Vinny jumped up and tried to lick her hands: 'For god's sake, Hoody; what are *you* doing here?'

'Culture clash!' Paul Grey laughed. He glanced from Miss Jennings' hastily retreating figure to Hoody's pale, scowling face. 'Two worlds collide!'

'What's funny?' Hoody sulked. He had his tough image to protect.

'You!' Carly insisted. He definitely looked like something Miss Jennings wouldn't like to meet after dark.

'Me? What about *her*? "Goodness!",' he mocked, throwing both hands in the air and imitating a high, posh old-lady voice. ' "Keep away! Don't touch me, you ruffian!" '

'Never the twain . . .' Paul murmured. 'But never mind. Carly, Hoody was hanging round Beech Hill like a spare part . . .'

'I wasn't!'

'Yes, you were, Hood. Anyway, I volunteered him to come out here and help you.' Carly's dad thrust a roll of black bin-bags at her, then made his way into Scottie's stable.

'Help me do what?' What were the bags for?

'Pull up all the ragwort in the paddock,' Paul said casually.

'In this heat?' Carly glanced up at the cloudless blue sky, the burning golden globe of the sun. 'All of it?'

Checking the horse's catheter, her dad nodded. 'The sooner the field's clear of all poisonous plants, the sooner we can put the horses out to graze again. Listen, you did a good job keeping the tube in place, but you can leave the rest to me now.'

'I want you to examine Holly and Meg first,' Carly insisted.

'Holly and Meg? First name terms already!' Paul's good mood showed that he was happy with Scottie's progress. He agreed to do as Carly asked, quickly moving next door to check the chestnut mare with stethoscope and thermometer.

'She seems pretty sound,' he reported. 'Though feeding the foal and staying outside in this heat has obviously taken it out of her. There's a slight infection in this left ear; probably caused by a mite. See this waxy discharge?'

Carly leaned forward and nodded.

'We'll take a specimen on a swab and check it under the microscope. Meanwhile, a dab or two of benzene hexachloride should do the trick.'

'What about Meg?' She was impatient for the verdict on the young foal, who had nuzzled close to her while Paul examined her mother. Her soft black muzzle rubbed against Carly's palm, then she gave her a shove with the flat of her nose.

'Meg has an eye infection.' Her dad took a pencil-torch from his bag and shone it in the foal's dark eyes. 'Probably conjunctivitis. It happens when pollen dust gets into the eye, especially in hot weather.'

'Is it serious?' Carly stroked the foal, then gently picked spiky burrs out of her short black mane.

'It could be if we don't treat it. It'll need antibiotic ointment around the lid, once we've bathed the whole area in warm saline solution . . .'

'I'll do that!' She jumped in with an offer she thought he couldn't refuse.

Grinning, Paul took his daughter by the shoulders, turned her round and marched her out of the stable. 'Paddock!' he ordered in a jerky, mechanical voice. He shot a mock-stern glance at a still-scowling Hoody and his hot mongrel dog. 'Tall yellow weed . . . ragwort . . . pull up by roots . . . stuff into bags, OK!'

4

'Six and seven!' Steve Winter brought two more pet carriers into the prep room.

Carly wrote down the numbers in black felt-tip on bright yellow tags and stuck them to the carriers. Behind the small, wire-mesh doors, two feral cats arched their backs and spat. 'Is that all?' she asked.

The inspector nodded. 'That's it for today. It's taken me more than an hour to trap this lot. They've got the run of the allotment, and there are dozens of places for them to hide. Once they get under the sheds and into the greenhouses, there's no way I can reach them.'

Seven cats in seven carriers hissed and yowled to be let out. 'What a racket!' Mel said as she hurried down the corridor wheeling a metal trolley.

'Shall I try feeding them?' Carly suggested as a way of keeping them quiet. To her, the wide-eyed, skinny creatures all looked in need of a good square meal.

Steve shook his head. 'No. Paul and Liz have a busy morning ahead of them. The four males will have to be neutered and the three females need spaying. So no food until after their ops, worse luck.'

'Not to mention tipping their ears and giving them their jabs,' Liz added. She came in buttoning her white coat and reaching for surgical gloves, opening the first cage in the row. She lifted out a mostly white cat with black marking over her ears and eyes.

'She looks like a bandit!' Carly smiled at Liz's squirming patient and took her from the vet while she prepared equipment for the anaesthetic: 'Listen, I know you don't like being here, but it's for your own good, honest!'

'Have you seen your father lately?' Holding a syringe close to the light, Liz checked the level of clear pre-med fluid.

'Talking to the police.' Carly had last seen him in reception with a young female police officer. He'd been passing on information about Scottie, Holly and Meg.

'We've got a definite cruelty case on our hands,' he'd been telling her. 'Our inspector, Steve Winter, is driving over there later to take photographs of the condition of the horses and begin the documentation. We were called out yesterday by Miss Jennings, a neighbour. I don't know her first name, I'm afraid. In fact, I'm pretty sure she won't want to be called as a witness; a nervous type, living alone and so on. But we plan to go ahead and prosecute in any case. When we finally get hold of the owners, that is.'

Was it only yesterday that they'd been called out to the horses? It seemed ages ago. Carly watched the white bandit-cat grow sleepy from the pre-med injection. Then, as soon as her eyes closed, Liz moved in with electric clippers to shave her leg and connect her up to the anaesthetic. Soon she was stretched out on the operating table, ready to be spayed.

Yes, yesterday! Her aching back and sore hands were the proof. She and Hoody had pulled up acres of ragwort; or that was how it had felt. They'd filled three black sacks with the stuff. Hoody had gone home to Beacon Street with the back of his neck sunburned and his jeans and trainers covered in bright green grass stains. His sister, Zoe, would have a fit, he said.

But he'd also said he might be back to help again this morning. He was a glutton for punishment; he said so himself.

Carly nipped to the door of the prep room and glanced out to see if Hoody had arrived. There was no sign of his tall, thin figure leaning against the door, nor of Vinny sitting with his pink tongue lolling in the heat. Another baking hot day, she told herself, glimpsing the blue sky beyond the block of flats opposite.

'Steve, could you ask Mel to come and give me a hand?' Liz was already well into the operation. 'And Carly, ask Bupinda to reschedule some of my appointments later this morning.'

They swung through the doors and left her to it.

'When are you going out to Greenacres?' Carly asked Steve, anxious to pin him down before she collared the receptionist.

'That's my next job,' he told her, catching the red-

43

haired nurse's attention in Treatment Room 1. 'Why? Do you want to come?'

'Yep. Me and Hoody. Watch out, here he comes now!'

The main door swung open and Hoody charged in, Vinny close on his heels. 'Emergency!' he yelled, kicking the inner door open and spying Paul still talking to the policewoman. Whatever he was carrying struggled and squawked in his arms.

'In here!' Paul reacted quickly, but without panicking. He made straight for the nearest treatment room. 'What have you got for us today, Hoody?'

'Duck! Found it in the park!' he gasped. '. . . Ow!'

The mallard had twisted his shiny green head and stabbed his abductor's hand with his beak. Hoody almost let go, but managed to hang on as wings flapped and feathers flew.

'Yuck, where did all this gunge come from?' Carly ran to lend a hand. She pinned the beating wings to the bird's sides and found her hands covered with smelly black slime.

'It's oil. You know that fair that's just been to the park?' Hoody was able let go of the mallard at last as Paul moved in.

'So?' At first, Carly didn't get the connection. She watched her dad calm the bird and ease one wing out to examine the coating of filthy oil on his breast.

'The fairground guys packed up last night. They must have left a plastic oilcan behind the football hut; you know, one of those gallon containers?'

'I know.' Carly was growing worried; the poor mallard was covered from head to foot in the black mess.

'It looks like it tipped over during the night and trickled into the ditch that runs into the lake. Vin and me came through there on our way here and found the duck slipping and sliding about in the ditch . . .' Hoody tailed off, staring down at his own hands and T-shirt.

'I know, and you couldn't just leave him!' Carly finished his sentence for him. She glanced up at the black marks all over his face and clothes. 'Zoe's gonna kill you!' she grinned.

'You only die once,' Hoody muttered. He sponged his T-shirt with the chemical that Paul had used to begin cleaning the bird's feathers with. The oil stains faded but refused to disappear.

'You only *live* once!' Carly insisted on getting it right.

'Nah. Believe me; you only *die* once. My sister already went mad when I showed up last night.' Hoody made a throttling motion, hands to his own throat. 'So what?'

'So you're still coming up to Greenacres this morning?' Carly wanted to know. She saw that Steve was ready to leave.

'Greenacres!' Paul heard the name and looked up. 'Listen, tell Steve to hang on until I've sorted this chap out!'

The mallard sat quietly now, letting himself be sponged and cleaned. His chest feathers were puffed out to dry, his beady eyes blinked under the strong overhead light.

'Holybridge Bird Sanctuary has a special infra-red unit to take care of oil-spillage victims,' Paul explained. 'He'll need to spend a few days recovering there before we put him back into the park.'

'I'll fetch a box,' Carly offered. She paused in the doorway. 'So, are you coming or not?' she asked Hoody.

'To pull up more weeds?' He turned down the

corners of his mouth and shrugged. Apart from the stripe of sunburn across the back of his neck, Hoody's skin had managed to stay paper-white despite the weeks of wall-to-wall sun.

'No!' Carly gave him one last chance. 'To help look after the horses!'

'What do you mean, look after?'

'Someone has to feed them and water them, don't they? Then they need ointment and eyedrops. Not to mention brushing and grooming! Who's gonna do that if we don't?'

Hoody frowned and glanced at Paul.

'She's right,' he confirmed. 'We have to look after them up there until we track down the owners, or until we find somewhere else for them to stay. And I don't want to move the grey horse until he's stronger, which won't be for a day or two at least. I'm coming over to check how he is after morning surgery.'

'But I don't even *like* horses!' Hoody complained. He put the oily cloth he'd been using in the bin, then wiped his hands on his jeans.

'So you're not coming?' she challenged, ready to flounce off. It wasn't the horses that Hoody didn't like; it was the big houses and fancy gardens, the four-wheel drives and the people looking down their noses.

'I never said that!' he retorted, unpredictable as ever. He was first across the waiting room and into Steve's van. 'Get a move on!' he called to Carly. 'At this rate we're *never* gonna get there!'

'Dad says we can feed this to Holly and Meg.' As soon as Steve had pulled up at the gates of Greenacres, Carly went to lug a paper sack out of the back of the van.

'What is it?' Hoody unfolded his long legs from his sitting position next to Vinny in the back of the van. He'd been hunched up for the long journey, which had included a stop to drop off the mallard at the bird sanctuary. He creaked out stiffly and stretched.

'Bran.' She staggered under the weight of the sack. 'I wanted to put the horses straight out into the paddock again, but Dad says he wants a farrier to come and take a look at their feet. Anyway, bran's best for them while they're getting over heatstroke.'

Taking one end of the sack, Hoody stumbled over the stile with Carly and up the bramble-strewn footpath. 'What about the grey horse?'

'No food, just water until Dad's examined him. Hey,

this is heavy!' The morning was as hot as ever; no breeze, no clouds to cool things down.

'Pity the front gate's locked,' Hoody grumbled as they climbed the fence into the paddock and hoisted the sack of food with them. Vinny slid under a gap, while Steve strode down the path after them, camera at the ready.

'There *is* a side gate.' Carly remembered Miss Jennings' surprise entrance of the day before. 'But to be honest, I don't know exactly how to get to it.' By now, they'd staggered up the slope to the gate of the paddock and had almost reached the stable yard. Carly could see Holly's head poking eagerly over her door, ears pricked. She seemed glad to see them after her night cooped up in the stall. Forgetting the weight of the sack, Carly dropped her end and ran to say hi.

'Uhh!' Hoody fell forward against the sack, arms almost pulled out of their sockets. Vinny yelped and scrambled out from under it just in time. ' "Hi, Holly!" ' Hoody mimicked a cutesy voice. ' "Hi, Meg! Hi, Scottie!" '

Carly ignored him. 'You look great!' she told the chestnut mare. The horse's eyes were brighter and the discharge from her ear had cleared up after just one application of the benzene solution. True, she was still an untidy mess, with grass seeds in her mane and tangles in her long tail. And little Meg was covered in grey dust, her coat matted with burrs. But that's what Carly and Hoody were here to sort out, with a grooming kit brought over from Beech Hill.

'Don't do anything until I've taken the photographs,' Steve warned. 'I need evidence of neglect.'

'In here.' Hoody led him quietly into Scottie's stable. 'This horse was the worst by far. He couldn't even stand up.'

'Well, he's on his feet now, so things are looking up.' Steve moved slowly towards the big grey. He studied him in silence then came out with a theory. 'I think I've seen this horse before. Not here at Greenacres; somewhere else.' Taking in the bony frame and lacklustre eyes, the bad saddle sore on Scottie's back and the split feet, he shook his head, 'Nope, forget it.'

'No, hang on. Where did you think you'd come across him?' Hoody persisted.

'It'll sound a bit off the wall if I tell you.' Steve was shaking his head and choosing a good angle to take his first shot. 'But I think it was at Worcester race course a couple of years back.'

'Race course?' Carly tuned in from the next door stable. She came to listen and watch.

'A steeplechase meeting. You see the dappled, smoky blue effect on his flanks and backside?'

Hoody and Carly both nodded.

'That colour's called blue roan. The horse I'm thinking of was a roan too; about sixteen and a half hands high, with the same white mane and tail.'

'Dad said Scottie could be a thoroughbred,' Carly recalled. 'Maybe what you're saying isn't so far-fetched.'

'Sir Walter ... something.' Steve only half-remembered the name. 'I put a fiver on him to win, but he came in third.'

'Sir Walter who?' Hoody asked sharply. Scottie had walked up to him and started to nudge him in the chest. Horse slobber mingled with the grass and oil stains on his seemingly one and only T-shirt.

'I don't know. I've just got Sir Walter in my head.' Steve moved up close and took a picture of the neglected saddle sore.

'Could it be Sir Walter Scott?' Hoody muttered.

Carly's mouth fell open and she stared at him. At times like this, Hoody amazed her.

'You know; the guy who wrote the Braveheart-type books,' he went on. 'Sir Walter Scott – Scottie. It's gotta be the same horse; it's obvious!'

'How did a top-class steeplechaser end up in this state?' Bill Foster, the blacksmith, asked the question still on everyone's minds. He and Paul Grey had arrived together. Now the farrier stood bent over with his back to Scottie, the horse's huge foot cupped in his broad hand.

Steve took close-up photographs of the deep cracks running vertically up the hoof.

'Severely malnourished, dehydrated, with possible damage to internal organs, grass cracks on all four hooves, untreated saddle sores . . .' Paul Grey began the list. 'Who knows what else after we've examined him thoroughly?'

'And all three horses left without shade or water in temperatures in the high eighties.' Steve had filled out the forms with the details needed to prove neglect.

As the three men stood discussing the case, Hoody and Carly worked with rakes and bucket, mucking out the mare and foal's stable. Meanwhile, Holly stood in one corner, munching her way through a bowl of bran, Meg sat quietly by the door in the sunshine.

'Do you want me to put clips in these hooves?' the blacksmith asked Paul. 'They stop the cracks from getting any worse. Then we put shoes on him in the normal way.'

Carly's dad gave the go-ahead. 'My next job is to get in touch with Sedgewood to see if they have room for three extra horses.'

Hoody stopped raking fresh straw across the floor, while Carly dumped the bucket of muck in the yard. Sedgewood City Farm was a place on the outskirts of town where they took some of the rescue animals from Beech Hill. They both knew it and listened carefully to Paul's future plans for Scottie, Holly and Meg.

'I know they're pretty full at the moment, but it's worth giving Geoff Best a ring. I wouldn't want to move the horses before the weekend in any case. Until then, we'll have to keep on taking it in turns to drive over here and keep an eye on them,' he told Steve. 'It's best if we keep them in at night and turn them out early in the day; the chestnut and the foal at least. Then we bring them in again before the sun reaches its height, and out at grass again for a couple of hours in the cool of the evening. Scottie here had better stay in on a ration of bran three times a day until he's fully convalesced.'

'Sounds like hard work,' Bill muttered, fetching a bag of clips from his car and clinking across the yard with it. He was young, with wavy red hair and skin that freckled in the sun. His bare arms were strong and smooth.

'We don't mind hard work!' Carly told him earnestly. 'Just so long as all three horses get better!'

'Good for you.' The blacksmith took out his hammer and a handful of the strong metal clips. He lifted one of Scottie's back hooves once more and began to drive in a clip with even, steady blows. 'But you can be sure of one thing.'

'What's that?' Carly winced, though the horse seemed not to mind.

Bill Foster smiled wryly and carried on hammering. 'The owners won't thank you for all this TLC you're lavishing on their animals; not when they get Steve's summons landing on their doormat!'

5

'Phew!' Carly brought Rusty in from his walk in the park. She unclipped the German shepherd's lead. While he investigated the disinfectant smell of the empty waiting-room floor, she took a leaflet from the rack and fanned her face.

'Good, I'm glad you found time to take him this morning!' Paul smiled at her, one hand supporting the phone, the other jotting notes into his diary.

'*He* took *me!*' she admitted. Her arms ached from trying to hold him back. 'Whoever gives Rusty a home will need to take him to training classes.'

'Just give him to Hoody for a couple of days!' Mel suggested as she passed through with a cat carrier in each hand. She grinned at Vinny walking obediently to heel as his owner slouched in and slumped down on a bench. Hoody blushed at the compliment and stared at his filthy trainers.

Meanwhile, Rusty picked up the scent of cats and made a dash at them. Mel slipped through the door just in time.

'Put that dog in his kennel before he starts World War Three!' Paul ordered. Then he got through on the phone. 'Hello, Geoff? Paul Grey here. How are you fixed for stable space at the moment? . . . Yep, I'd heard you were under pressure. The thing is, I'm looking for a temporary home for three abandoned horses we found out at Holybridge a couple of days ago . . .'

Keeping her fingers crossed, Carly took Rusty along the corridor into the kennel building at the back of the rescue centre. She made sure that his bowl was full of clean water, then took time to look in on Mitch, the little black-and-white terrier who had been brought in with heatstroke two days earlier. He trotted up to the door of his kennel, eyes bright, tail wagging, poking a wet black nose through the wire mesh.

'Home for you soon!' she promised, hoping that Mitch's careless owner had learned his lesson once and for all.

'. . . What's today? Thursday.' Carly's dad checked his diary and spoke to Geoff Best at the city farm as she went back to Reception. 'Well, I'd want to move them over to you on Saturday at the earliest. How would that be?'

'It's looking good.' Steve had come out of the office while she'd been dealing with Rusty, and now gave Hoody and Carly the thumbs-up sign. 'Who's ready to drive over to Greenacres with me?'

'Me!' Hoody shot to his feet, making Vinny jump.

'For someone who doesn't like horses, you're pretty keen all of a sudden,' Carly teased. She followed him into the van, winding down the window for what she knew would be another slow, hot journey.

He sniffed and ignored her. 'Steve, what happens if these owners show up before we move the horses? Do they get to keep them while we get ready to take them to court?'

'Good point.' Carly hadn't thought of this.

The inspector filtered into traffic heading for the city centre. 'No. If they come back, I serve the summons and we take the animals to a safe place pending the court case. It's just the same as if it was a dog or a cat we were dealing with,' he explained. 'In that situation, we'd be able to keep them at Beech Hill in the isolation unit. With horses, we need somewhere like Sedgewood.'

'So there's nothing wrong with trying to track down the Martyns as quickly as we can?' Carly had gone off on her own tack, staring absent-mindedly at the bright billboards advertising cars and mobile phones.

'No. The quicker I can serve the summons, the sooner we can bring them to court.' Steve glanced sideways at her. 'Why?'

'Nothing. Well, I'll tell you later.' Privately, she'd made up her mind to call in at Dower House for another talk with Miss Jennings. She decided it would be better to go alone, without Steve or Hoody, so as not to scare the old lady off.

'I was reading this book,' Hoody remarked casually after a few minutes of silence, as they crept along through the slow traffic. They were in a tiled tunnel lit by a strip of fluorescent light, cruising under the city centre. 'About how to train horses.'

Carly didn't say anything. When she first knew

him, the idea of Hoody reading any kind of book might have surprised her. These days, she'd learned when not to show it. Like now. His face as he sat hunched in the back of the van was fixed in serious lines.

'You don't need to use force. It's all about body language.' Relaying what he'd read to Steve, Hoody's voice was eager. 'And about how you talk to them.'

'Horse whispering,' Steve nodded. 'An American idea. It's all the rage.'

'What do you reckon?'

'I reckon, yeah, it must be right.' Steve threaded his way into the North Wootton lane. 'It works with other animals. Why not horses?'

Hoody the Horse Whisperer. Carly conjured up a novel picture of the kid who didn't even like horses talking softly into Scottie's, Holly's or little Meg's ear. Weirder things had happened, she guessed.

But as they approached Greenacres – the quiet lane and the empty house – her mind switched to other things. 'Drop me here, please,' she said to Steve at the gate to Dower House. 'I'll meet you up at the stables in half an hour, OK?'

* * *

'You'd like me to tell you Scottie's story?' Miss Jennings repeated the phrase Carly had used. She kept her standing on the doorstep, breathing in the scent from the yellow roses that climbed over the front porch.

'Yes please.' Careful to mind her manners, Carly waited patiently. Carly the Old Lady Whisperer. Don't use force, don't scare them with your body language, talk nicely.

Miss Jennings blinked nervously. She wore her grey hair curled prettily around her thin, lined face, a touch of pink lipstick, little pearl earrings. 'Are you alone?' she asked Carly.

'Yes. Steve Winter and Hoody – my friend, Jon Hood – have gone on up to the stables. I wondered if there was anything else you could tell us that would help.' Beside the old lady, Carly felt too glossy and bright, with her black, shiny hair, her sky-blue T-shirt and tanned, bare limbs.

'I don't know . . . I'm not sure . . .' Miss Jennings' grey eyes flickered uncertainly. 'If the Martyns find out that this has anything at all to do with me . . . I'm very much afraid that they would make my life a complete misery!'

'Why? What could they do?' Carly was puzzled. After all, Kingsley and Olivia Martyn were the ones who were in the wrong.

'They could evict me from my home for a start.' The old lady made a clean breast of what was worrying her. 'They own Dower House and I pay them rent.'

'I see!' Carly didn't probe.

Miss Jennings' confidences continued regardless. 'My father used to own all the property and he was the one who built the new house, Greenacres. But in the nineteen fifties he fell into debt and had to sell.

'The Martyn family – that is, Kingsley's parents – bought everything very cheaply, with the unwritten proviso laid down by my father just before he died that they must continue to rent Dower House to me for as long as I chose to stay here.' She sighed and shook her head. 'Kingsley's father stuck to the agreement while he was alive, but when the old man finally died five years ago, and Kingsley moved in with his wife, things changed. Since then, they've made it very clear at every opportunity that they want me out.'

'And you've nowhere to go?' Carly suddenly felt

very sorry for the defenceless old lady. And she saw how much courage it had taken for her to take action on behalf of Scottie and the other two horses. 'Look, I'll leave you alone from now on,' she promised. 'And I'll make sure that Steve doesn't mention your name in the papers for the court case.'

'You're actually taking the Martyns to court?' Miss Jennings' hand flew to her cheek. 'Goodness!'

'Don't worry.' Carly backed away from the door. 'You won't have to give evidence. I'm sure Steve has plenty of information without that.'

'And justice will be done?'

She nodded. 'We hope so.'

The old lady followed Carly down the path. 'I may be old-fashioned, but I do believe in British justice,' she murmured. 'If a wrong has been committed, I would want to help put it right.'

'Yes, but you've done enough.' Eager to let her off the hook, Carly was already through the creaking iron gate. 'And since you don't have a holiday address for the Martyns, there's not much more you can do.'

'But you wanted Scottie's story?' Miss Jennings overrode Carly and went back to the original question. 'Scottie is Sir Walter Scott; Joel Kingsley's horse.'

Carly stopped in her tracks and turned back. Hoody and Steve had been right. 'Was he a racehorse?'

The old lady nodded. 'Joel is a first rate rider over hurdles, and Scottie was a horse with a great future when the Martyns bought him as a three year old, just after they moved in to Greenacres. The son was seventeen and Claire, the daughter, was just thirteen. She was largely overlooked, poor child. I suppose it was because she wasn't gifted or ambitious like her older brother.'

'Didn't she have her own horse?' Carly asked, wondering about Holly and Meg in the stable.

'Not for years. She would have liked one dearly, I know. She would come here to see me in the early days and pour out all her troubles; how her mother and father put all their energy into making Joel a success on Sir Walter Scott, driving him to novice meetings, getting the best trainers and so on. They seemed to think that poor Claire had no talent for riding. Then they sent her away to school. Meanwhile, Joel was doing well, and all was going according to plan.'

'Then what?' Carly picked up the old lady's hesitation.

'I'm not sure exactly, but several bad things happened earlier this year. I heard rumours that Claire had fallen ill with a mystery ailment which meant she was having difficulty finishing her final year at school. She was due to return to Greenacres this summer in any case. And at last, Kingsley and Olivia seemed to soften and were ready to buy her a horse.'

'That's where Holly and Meg come in?' Carly prompted.

'Yes. The mare was in foal when they bought her, though they probably didn't realise it at the time. Kingsley isn't particularly knowledgeable about horses, and his wife certainly isn't. Joel was the expert.'

'So why didn't the son pick up the fact that Holly was pregnant?' Forgetting about the hot sun beating down on their bare heads, Carly was drawn further and further into the Martyns' complex family history.

'Because by that time Joel and his parents had had a very bad argument.' Miss Jennings leaned closer, as if afraid that someone might overhear. 'It was over Scottie. They had taken the horse to a race meeting in February and there'd been an accident. Scottie was lamed. Kingsley blamed Joel. I suppose things were said in the heat of the moment.

'The end result was that Joel threatened to take himself and the horse away from Greenacres to train and work at a stables near Worcester. From what I hear, Kingsley forbade him. He said Scottie belonged to him, not Joel, and that, lame or not, the horse must stay where he was. Now, I'm not sure whether it was Joel who stormed out and never returned, or if Kingsley actually banned his son from the premises, as some people say.'

'So, anyway, Joel disappears and a new horse comes at more or less the same time.' Carly pieced together the events of the spring. 'So what happened to Claire?'

'That's what no one knows!' Miss Jennings' voice fell away to a sad murmur. 'She never came home from school, she never saw her beautiful chestnut mare.

'And of course, without Joel, both horses were badly looked after. For a time, the Martyns employed a local girl called Sarah Fenton to muck out the stables. But Sarah never rode the horses. And it seems Holly was unbroken. Kingsley had bought her without her even so much as having had a saddle on her back. Then of course the foal was born. The girl stopped coming.

Scottie went downhill very rapidly, so that to look at him now you would never suppose that he and Joel used to win races up and down the country.'

A frown set into Carly's features as the story unravelled. 'So it reached the point when Claire didn't show up as she was supposed to, Joel had vanished without trace, and the girl who was meant to look after the horses stopped coming. Then the Martyns themselves go off to Greece!'

Miss Jennings nodded. 'Late last week. I can only think that they made an arrangement to have Scottie, Holly and the foal looked after in their absence, but that somehow, unbeknown to them, the arrangement fell through.'

Carly thought this was too kind. 'Or else, they never even bothered to contact anyone about the horses!' she muttered. 'They sound the sort who *would* just go off on holiday and leave their animals to fend for themselves!' Selfish, cruel, unthinking people who always put themselves first. 'I take it you never saw anyone call?'

'No one I recognised.' Miss Jennings shaded her eyes with her thin hands, pursed her lips, then offered a hesitant remark. 'I did see a young woman stop by last Sunday afternoon. Of course, I see everything from my house; I notice any car that turns down the lane, and especially one which stops at Greenacres.'

Carly nodded eagerly. 'This woman; what did she look like?'

'Young,' Miss Jennings said hazily. 'With fair hair. She was driving a small silver car; a sports car I suppose you would call it. She stopped at the gates, but when she found them locked, she gave up and went back to her car. She seemed nervous; almost glad that there was no one at home. It didn't take her long to turn her car in the lane and speed back to the main road. Before I had time to think, or to go and tell her that the Martyns were away, she was gone.'

'And you don't remember anything else about her?' Carly prompted. She was ready now to run up to the house and pass on to Steve and Hoody what she'd just learned. But this last question was important. 'Silver sports car. Fair hair. Anything else?'

'No, not about her,' the old lady said. She thought hard, shading her eyes and narrowing them to a frown. 'But there was one other thing.'

'What was that?' It might be vital; this final piece of

information squeezed out of well-meaning, kindly but frightened Miss Jennings.

'She had a dog in the car with her.'

'Right.' Carly was disappointed. 'What sort of dog?' she asked, as she set off up the lane.

'A golden retriever,' came the clear, prompt answer. 'Sitting there large as life in the passenger seat, with the top down. I could hear it barking its head off as they went by.'

6

With a steady hand Hoody squeezed antibiotic drops from a white plastic bottle into the corner of Meg's eye.

Carly and Steve looked on quietly.

'Once we've finished with the lotions and potions, we can put Scottie out with Holly and Meg,' Steve said. 'Paul reckons he's well enough to spend a couple of hours in the paddock before the sun gets too hot. It means we can gradually take him off the bran and get him eating normally before we ship them off to Sedgewood at the weekend.'

'Did Geoff Best finally say yes?' Carly took firm

hold of Holly's headcollar as the mare kept a wary eye on what Hoody was doing to her foal. 'Easy!' she murmured. The anxious mother shifted and stamped her feet.

'He says they'll make room by keeping the donkeys out at night. Which means moving the deer into the field where they normally keep cows, and the cows in with the sheep, and so on.' Steve took the bottle from Hoody and handed him some cream to rub around the foal's eye. 'It's good for Meg to get plenty of handling at this age,' he advised. 'Put the headcollar on now and bring her along with the mare, while I lead Scottie out.'

Together they prepared the three horses to be led to the paddock behind the house.

'You're quiet,' Hoody muttered to Carly as they waited at the gate. 'What's the problem?'

'You can talk!' she retorted. When it came down to it, Hoody wasn't exactly the world's greatest conversationalist.

'Yeah, but you're usually jumping in with the questions.' He shot her a shrewd glance. 'What did the old woman say?'

'I'll tell you later.' Carly was still sorting out in her

own mind how best to protect Miss Jennings. 'She did mention that Holly's never been ridden, though.' Letting the mare off the lead rope, they watched her trot down the slope.

Then Hoody released Meg, who kicked out her spindly back legs and cantered after her mother. 'Weird,' he murmured. 'Who would buy a horse and not ride it?'

'It's a long story,' she sighed, waiting for Steve to lead Scottie into the paddock. She was pleased to note that not a single stalk of ragwort had survived their afternoon of back-breaking work. Scottie seemed happy to be out in the fresh air and strong enough to take steady, even steps across the grass. Though he was still thin after the months of neglect, his eyes were brighter and he carried his head higher than when they had first seen him in the heat haze, starving and thirsty and on the point of collapse.

'What do you know about lunging and stuff?' Hoody broke into Carly's thoughts. He had crouched down beside Vinny, pulled a stalk of grass and was chewing the juicy end as he spoke. A fly settled on his pale cheek and he flicked it off.

'Not much.' She said she thought it might have

something to do with a long rope and making the horse trot in a circle. 'Why?'

'I'll tell you later,' he replied, grinning at her then giving Vinny the word to make his way back to the van. 'C'mon, Carly, what are you waiting for?'

'This here is a lunge cavesson, and this is a lunge rein.' Hoody held up two dusty items which he'd dug out of the tack-room at the rear of Scottie's stable.

It was Thursday afternoon. Paul had dropped Hoody and Carly off at Greenacres and gone on to a call at the bird sanctuary. 'A lunge *cave* . . . what?' Carly was puzzled. What was Hoody up to now?

'*Cavesson*. I read it in a book.'

'What book?'

'A horse book from the library. "The Complete Horse Encyclopaedia". See these rings on the nose band?'

She nodded and held on to Meg as he'd requested. Scottie watched with interest from the far side of the field.

'Well, you clip the rein on to the rings once you've put the cavesson on like a normal headcollar.' Hoody went ahead and demonstrated on Holly. 'Then you let out the rein like so!'

She watched as he eased the soft webbing rope out to about half its full length of ten metres or so. Holly shook her head and flicked her ears. She took a step or two and found that the rein pulled taut.

'I'm gonna use this free end of the rein to flick her backside, see!' Hoody was getting into the whole idea. When he threw the loose end against Holly's rump, she reacted by quickening her pace and breaking into a trot. Restrained by the cavesson and lunge rein, she paced out a wide circle around the top end of the paddock.

Carly held tight to an excited Meg. The little foal was eager to follow her mother, pulling at her headcollar and kicking out. 'I'm impressed!' she confessed.

' "Lunging teaches a horse obedience." ' Hoody quoted from the book he'd read. He flicked Holly again, murmured the words, 'Walk on!', and watched her pick up speed. ' "It teaches her to go forward from the indications of the whip while establishing the habit of obedience to the voice." '

'How old is this horse manual?' She laughed at the quaint language. 'A hundred years?'

'Ancient. Practically prehistoric. So what? It still

works, doesn't it?' He tugged gently on the rein and told Holly 'Whoa!'

'Excellent!' Carly felt like clapping, but she had her hands full. Meg head-butted her and almost knocked her off her feet. 'Is it difficult?' She wanted to know how Hoody managed to control the length of the lunge rein at the same time as flicking the other end accurately against Holly's trotting rump.

'Nah, dead easy,' he insisted, switching the rein to his right hand and setting Holly off again in the opposite direction. 'The book makes it sound complicated, but the real thing's simple. The horse does it for you, see. Look at her; she's brilliant!'

Carly nodded. The sun on Holly's coat gave it a sheen that it hadn't had before. She picked up her newly shod feet and held out her flowing tail so that it streamed behind her. Round and round she went to Hoody's command, cavesson rings jingling, hooves striking the hard stones that lay on the surface of the rough paddock. 'He's good, isn't he?' she said to Vinny, who sat patiently at the gate.

Vinny wagged his thin tail and stretched his wide mouth. If Carly hadn't known better, she would have sworn that the dog was smiling.

* * *

'More work!' Hoody insisted. The first thing he did when they went back to Greenacres early next morning was to dig out the cavesson and lunge rein again.

Steve shook his head. 'There's no stopping him once he's started!'

Grinning, Carly went to lean on the paddock fence and enjoy the display. 'If I know Hoody, he'll have a saddle on Holly before long!' She'd seen a couple, as dirty and disused as the rest of the tack, hanging from sturdy racks in a dark corner of the tack-room.

Hoody overheard as he led the mare into the field. 'What's wrong with that?'

'Nothing!' Carly laughed.

'Take it easy, that's all.' Steve warned him not to rush Holly. 'I know these horse whisperers claim they can get on the back of a horse in twenty minutes, but you don't want to go trying it without a round pen and plenty of supervision. You have to know horses and you have to be quite sure of what you're doing, OK?'

Grudgingly Hoody promised that he wouldn't attempt to put a saddle on Holly and ride her. 'Thanks, Steve!' he muttered, as the inspector left them to it and went to answer his mobile phone ringing from the pocket of his jacket which he'd left hanging on the stable door.

'It's only because he doesn't want you to hurt yourself,' Carly pointed out. She climbed the fence and went across the field to intercept Meg, who was trotting towards them. She would hold on to the foal while he worked the mare. 'And because Holly is part of the evidence in a cruelty case, remember. She isn't even our horse!'

'I'm not doing her any harm, am I?' He frowned as he let out the rein and set Holly trotting in a tight circle. Today she seemed more willing; she needed fewer flicks from the end of the rope and seemed to understand Hoody's spoken commands.

'That's not the point.' Ready as always for a friendly argument, Carly glanced round when she heard Steve's footsteps returning across the yard. 'Who was that on the phone?' she asked.

'Your dad.' Steve was brisk and upbeat, filling them in before he drove on to his next call. 'The police just dropped by with the latest development.'

'About Scottie and co.?'

He nodded. 'More specifically, about the Martyns.

Someone at the station had the bright idea that they could be traced via their travel agent. So they checked the major companies who rent out villas in Greece, starting at the posh end of the market, and soon came up with the Martyns' destination. They're on Rhodes; in a village called Lindos. The police contacted the company rep on the island with a message for Olivia and Kingsley Martyn to get in touch.'

Carly listened carefully, one eye on Hoody who went on lunging Holly. The horse trotted neatly, stopped when he wanted her to, waited, then turned. 'Just what they want to hear . . . *not*!' She pictured the Martyns' lazy days on the beach coming to an abrupt end.

'Don't waste any sympathy,' Steve advised. Cruelty cases brought out a serious, determined streak in the ex-builder turned animal inspector. He rolled up his sleeves and squinted up at white clouds drifting across the sun. 'If the message gets through, and it means they have to cut short their holiday to get back here so we can serve a summons, it's no more than they deserve.'

'I know it,' Carly agreed. She too noticed the clouds. Perhaps the weather was breaking.

'And we'll get answers to our questions,' Steve

reminded her, reaching over the fence to stroke Meg. 'Like, what sort of people abandon horses in a heatwave?'

Like, what sort of parents argue with their son and send him packing? she thought to herself. *Like, what had happened to the daughter, Claire? Why hadn't she come back from school?* All those nagging questions which Carly had kept to herself since her long talk with Miss Jennings still needed answers too.

And the biggest one of all, as far as the lonely lady in the Dower House was concerned; *would Olivia and Kingsley Martyn put two and two together and get four? Would they realise that it was their neighbour who had called the rescue centre in the first place? That it was Miss Jennings who had called them to account for their cruel neglect of three wonderful creatures: the gifted steeplechaser, the proud, unbacked mare and her lively bay foal?*

'Rain before tomorrow.' Paul told Carly and Hoody the forecast as they drove through Holybridge. It was Friday evening, and his turn to check on Scottie, Holly and Meg. 'Thunderstorms for our area.'

The white clouds of early morning had gathered and turned grey, then purplish-greenish-blue. The atmosphere was muggy and stale. Tucked between Hoody's legs in the back of the car, Vinny looked miserable at the prospect of a storm.

'Let's hope we get the horses in before it starts.' Carly didn't fancy trying to catch them in the paddock during a full-scale downpour. Thunder and lightning scared her too.

'We need the rain . . . badly!' Her dad glanced out at the parched fields and hedgerows, then pulled into a petrol station to fill up. 'Two minutes!' he promised his uneasy passengers.

Leaning out of the window, Carly looked up beyond the station awning at the gloomy sky. The day at Beech Hill had been the usual whirl of feeding and walking, mopping and wiping, fetching and carrying of cats, a tortoise, two hamsters and a pet rat called Napoleon from waiting room to treatment room and from prep room into surgery. Hoody, on the other hand, had spent the day on the step of the football pavilion in Beech Hill Park, buried in his Complete Horse Encyclopaedia.

' "The backing process is best done for the first time in a confined space, where there is less risk of an accident",' he quoted from memory now. 'That means putting the saddle on in the stable.'

'You wish!' Carly gave him a quick grin. 'Well, who knows, maybe you can keep on working with Holly after we've moved them to the city farm.'

Glancing out of the window into the middle distance, Hoody nodded non-committally. 'Nice car,' he muttered, to change the subject.

'Where?' *Don't push it*, she thought. *He probably doesn't want to get his hopes up too far about him and Holly.*

'Just leaving.' He pointed to a low, silver car indicating to turn right on to the road.

Low and silver, with a black soft top. The top was down, in spite of the threatening clouds and the first drop or two of cold rain. A silver sports car. Carly looked again.

The driver was a woman. Carly had time to see that her fair hair was pulled back from her face with a shiny black and gold clasp. There was a flash of red finger nails, a gold watch on her wrist, but only the back of her head was visible before she drew out of the garage and drove off towards the city.

'Hey!' Carly whispered.

The sound of alarm in her voice made Vinny sit up and take notice.

'What?' Hoody stared after the speedy little car.

Red brake lights came on as the driver approached a bend, then the car disappeared. 'Nothing.' Carly sat back to wait for her dad, shoulders hunched, deep in thought. 'It's just something Miss Jennings told me, that's all.'

The three horses stood waiting at the paddock gate. Scottie's eyes rolled, his ears were back as he smelled rain and sensed the approaching thunder. Holly stayed protectively beside Meg, sheltering her from the wind that had got up as the clouds rolled towards their hill.

'We can still beat the storm if we're quick!' Paul Grey said. He'd parked by the gates of Greenacres and hurried up the overgrown footpath with Carly and Hoody. 'Where are the lead ropes to bring the horses in?'

'Hanging on a hook in Scottie's tack-room,' Hoody answered, while Carly set off at a run across the yard.

Wet drops splashed on to the dusty concrete. The air grew close and clammy. An unseen door banged.

Carly ran into the first stable and fumbled inside the tack-room for the ropes. 'They aren't here!' she called.

'Yeah, they are!' Hoody insisted. He came up close

behind her and felt for a light switch by the inner door.

Outside, the rain began to fall faster.

'See!' Carly stepped inside the tack-room and pointed to the empty hooks.

'They were there this morning. That's where I left them.' Looking round the small, stuffy room, Hoody tried to make sense of what had happened.

'Where are the saddles?' The racks in the corner were empty, shelves had been disturbed, bins kicked over. She turned to Hoody with a look of dismay. 'What's going on?'

'Don't look at me!' he yelled. '*I* didn't do it!'

'Hey, you two, cool it.' Paul had followed them and walked in on the row. He stood a plastic feed bin upright and systematically took in the chaotic scene.

Carly's heart beat madly. Except for a couple of old ropes lying coiled on the floor, the tack-room was bare.

'There's been a break-in,' her dad said calmly. 'The thieves must have taken everything they could lay their hands on. At least there's one good thing, though.'

'What?' Hoody and Carly asked. Where was the good news, for heaven's sake?

Paul spelt it out. 'The tack may have gone, God knows where. But at least the horses are safe!'

7

They used the frayed ropes left behind by the thieves to bring Scottie, Holly and Meg in from the field. Swirls of wind gusted against Carly's T-shirt and trousers, cold raindrops soaked through the thin cotton and splashed on to her bare arms and face.

'You get Meg!' Paul shouted above the wind and the first distant roll of thunder. 'They're all spooked by the weather, but if you can bring the foal in, Holly will probably follow!'

'I'll try!' she promised. Luckily the horses were wearing headcollars, so all she had to do was to slip the rope through a ring, secure it and lead Meg out of the field.

But it was easier said than done. As soon as she tried to corner the frightened foal in the top corner of the paddock, a flash of forked lightning split the black sky in two. Meg whinnied and reared, then darted straight at Carly, who had to step quickly to one side. Two seconds later, a crash of thunder sent all three horses careering crazily to the bottom of the slope.

'Let me try with Holly,' Hoody yelled. The rain and wind had turned him into a dripping wet, scrawny scarecrow figure, stumbling, rope in hand, down the field.

A second streak of lightning darted earthwards, followed by a wild crack of thunder.

'Careful!' Carly pleaded. She knew Hoody wouldn't heed the danger of approaching a spooked horse in a storm.

True to form, he didn't hesitate. 'Easy, girl!' he said through gritted teeth as he drew near to Holly.

The mare was sheltering Meg from the force of the wind. Her ears were flat against her head, her nostrils flared. Every nerve in her body was alive to the chaos of the storm, every muscle bunched ready to gallop away.

'That's it; easy!' Hoody drew closer. He ignored the flashes of bright light, the cracks of thunder overhead. The coil of rope was looped over his shoulder as he stretched out a helping hand to take hold of Holly's headcollar.

She raised her head and edged away, rain streaming down her neck and turning her rich chestnut coat almost black. She flinched as she felt Hoody's hand take hold of the collar. The muscles in her shoulders quivered, but she didn't fight or flee.

'Easy!' he breathed as he slipped the rope through the ring and tied a knot. He nodded at Carly to move in on Meg. 'C'mon, let's get out of here!'

Quickly Carly slid in beside the trembling foal. In seconds she'd secured the rope and they were following Hoody and Holly up the slope. Out of the corner of her eye, across the rain-soaked field, she saw that her dad still kept his distance from a frightened Scottie.

'I'll wait to see if he follows you!' Paul yelled.

She nodded and went on, head down, water trickling into her eyes. They were through the gate and crossing the yard, then through the stable door, safe at last from the wind and rain.

'I'll go and help Dad!' she gasped, ready to dash out into the rain again as Hoody took Meg's rope from her.

'It's OK; relax. He made it.' Hoody pointed to the drenched figures of Paul and Scottie crossing the yard. 'They're all safe.'

The big grey thoroughbred plodded into his stable, coat steaming, breathing heavily. 'Well done, you two!' Paul called from next door.

For a few minutes, while the rain still pelted down and the thunder rolled, they did their best to rub the horses dry with fistfuls of straw. Then Paul decided they'd done all they could. 'The lightning's passed over,' he told them, coming into Holly and Meg's stable. 'Which means the horses should soon settle down. We'll leave them in overnight and be back first thing in the morning with a box. 'We'll have to force a lock on the yard gate, lead them out and drive them over to Sedgewood.'

Dropping her handful of straw, Carly sighed and agreed that it was time to go. Her body trembled from the soaking she'd received, her black hair hung in straggly rat's tails. And she noticed that Hoody and Paul were in an equally bad way. But at least Scottie, Meg and Holly were warm and dry.

'See you tomorrow,' she whispered, making the foal a special, deep bed in the driest corner of the stable. It was like tucking up a small child for the night as Meg snuggled into the straw, legs folded beneath her, huge brown eyes blinking sleepily up at her. *Good night, sleep tight. Mind the bugs don't bite.*

'Smell that!' Steve Winter breathed in the fresh scent of grass and earth after heavy rain.

It was Saturday morning; the day fixed to bring the Greenacres' horses over to Sedgewood City Farm.

The storm had cleared the air and put an end to the August heatwave. Summer's dusty, parched days were over.

'The stream's back!' Carly pointed to a channel of clear water trickling along the bed of a ditch that ran down the slope by the paddock fence. She smiled as she released little Meg into the field and watched her frisk alongside her mother who was grazing quietly after the upset of the previous day's storm.

'One last session out here for you,' Steve told Scottie.

He let the grey horse loose to eat grass, then turned to Hoody. 'Do you want to stay here and work with Holly while Carly and I pick up the horsebox?'

'I can't, can I?' Hoody shrugged and set off towards the gate. He'd been even quieter and more turned into himself than usual this morning.

'Why not?'

'No cavesson, no lunge rein,' he mumbled.

'I forgot.' Steve waited for Carly to slip through the gate, then closed it after her. 'What did the police say when you reported the break-in?' he asked her.

'They think it might link in with some other thefts from stables round here,' she told him. 'Last Tuesday, for instance, seven hundred pounds worth of stuff went from a place further up the North Wootton road.'

'Saddles and bridles,' Hoody chipped in. 'The same as here.'

'The police recommended installing cameras and warning signs,' Carly went on. 'Dad said that was definitely a case of shutting the stable door after the horse had bolted!'

Hoody grimaced. 'In other words, they haven't a clue who's breaking into these places!' He and Vinny climbed into their usual corner in the back of Steve's van.

Carly agreed. 'But you have to admit, we didn't give them many clues. We couldn't even tell them exactly when the break-in happened, or what went missing, or what it was worth!'

'OK, OK.' Hoody knew that it was pretty hopeless. 'It's just one more shock for the Martyns when they get back.'

'Which should be soon.' Taking a last, long-distance look at the three horses in the paddock as Steve set off slowly down the lane, Carly turned her attention to the task in hand. They had to collect the horsebox from Sedgewood, then drive back out for Scottie, Holly and Meg. By lunchtime, they should be away from Greenacres for good and safely settled in their temporary new home.

'I just hope they're easy to load.' Steve's recent difficulty in trapping allotment cats made him consider the stress connected with leading three horses up a ramp into a scary metal box on wheels.

'No problem!' Carly assured him. This morning there was a cool, light wind rustling through the trees at the side of the road, nice white clouds racing across the sky; she felt that nothing could possibly go wrong. 'With Hoody around to help, it'll be a breeze!'

'Wake me up when we get there!' Hoody grunted from the high cab of the horsebox. He put his feet up on the dashboard and closed his eyes.

They were riding in a huge truck, looking down on the hedges, rumbling along High Wootton road at twenty miles per hour. 'It feels like we're crawling!' Carly complained, impatient to get to Greenacres. 'Can't we go any faster?'

'This is as good as it gets, I'm afraid.' Unruffled, Steve chugged along. 'This engine is fifteen years old remember, and the bodywork isn't what you'd call in mint condition.'

The side panels of the horsebox were dented and rusty, the ramp at the back rattled and shook as they bounced along. But they were almost there. Carly spotted the stone gateway to Holybridge Bird Sanctuary and the few scattered houses that made up the village. Ahead, the road narrowed and the surface grew more uneven. Then, at last, there was Dower House and the lane they would turn up to reach the Martyns' place.

'Hi, Miss Jennings!' Carly leaned out of the window of the cab to wave at the old lady in her old-fashioned garden. She caught a strained look on her pale, lined face, and was surprised to see her quickly turn her back and slip inside the house, her pleated lilac skirt swinging out behind her as she disappeared.

For a moment, Carly felt like stopping to reassure her that she hadn't mentioned their conversation of a few days before. 'Don't worry!' she wanted to say, now that she understood the reasons behind Miss Jennings' nervousness. 'Olivia and Kingsley Martyn will never be able to prove that it was you who raised the alarm in the first place!'

But she'd already failed to reassure the Martyns' tenant. So what would be the point of stopping now?

'OK?' Steve queried. He'd lifted his foot off the accelerator pedal and slowed the truck to walking pace.

Carly nodded. 'Carry on,' she murmured, looking eagerly up the lane to where the white-and-black, mock Tudor house stood behind its tall iron gates.

The sides of the horsebox brushed the hawthorn hedges to either side of the lane, startling a thrush which flew up from the ditch and across their path.

Steve braked and turned the wheel, steering into the soft grass verge and just managing to pull back on to the track in time.

'Watch it!' Hoody grumbled, waking up with a start. 'Where are we? What happened?'

'We're there.' Carly had grabbed a handle to steady herself. 'There's the field, see!'

Hoody sat upright and let Vinny scramble on to the seat beside him. He scanned what they could see of the paddock from the lane. 'So where are they?'

The field looked deserted, rising to a ridge, then sloping away from the house on the hill. Carly frowned. 'Down at the far end, I guess.'

Waiting until Steve finally pulled up outside the drive, Hoody, Carly and Vinny jumped down from the cab. Recognising the way to the overgrown footpath, the dog scooted between their feet, leaped the stile and ran ahead. They saw his curved, thin tail bobbing between brambles and knee-high clumps of long grass and bright yellow dandelions.

'Slow down, Vin!' Carly called. 'Don't scare the horses!' She caught a glimpse of him scuttling under the paddock fence, then a clear view of him in the field itself.

'I don't get it.' Hoody shook his head. 'He never runs on like that!'

Picking her way through the brambles, Carly turned to frown back at him. 'Yeah, and where's he gone now?' she muttered, as the mongrel dog vanished over the near horizon.

'C'mon!' Hoody's face showed that he thought something was definitely wrong.

'Ouch!' she gasped, as he let go of a bramble and the thin, thorny branch whipped against her leg. She hobbled after him, across the ditch and over the fence into the field.

Then Vinny came bounding back into view, barking at the top of his voice. He ran towards them, turned and urged them to follow him over the crest of the hill and down the slope towards the stream.

'What's up, Vin?' Hoody ran until he reached the brow, Carly beside him. They were gasping for breath, scanning the hidden part of the paddock, expecting to see the three horses in some sort of trouble. Maybe Meg had fallen into the ditch and hurt her leg. Scottie and Holly would be standing by, waiting anxiously for help.

But no; that wasn't the problem.

'Where are they?' Hoody repeated his question, bending double to catch his breath.

Carly watched Vinny race around the edge of the field, into the ditch and out again, then charging up the slope towards them.

Empty! That's what he'd been trying to say; the horses weren't here in the paddock where they were supposed to be. He'd looked in every corner and come bounding back to tell them: Scottie, Holly and Meg had vanished!

8

The truth sank in slowly, after Carly, Hoody and Steve had walked the length and breadth of the Martyns' field. The horses had been stolen.

'I bet it's the same bunch who sneaked in yesterday and stole the tack!' Steve said. It was the obvious train of thought; opportunist thieves who'd staked out the place and cottoned on to the fact that Greenacres was shut-up and empty. They'd gone away and organised transport, come back the next day, broken the locks and stolen the horses.

The Beech Hill inspector explained his theory on

the phone to Paul, after he'd rung the police. 'It stands to reason,' he insisted. 'They poke around yesterday and snatch what they can carry there and then. But they're not just any old break-in merchants; they know about horses and they recognise a valuable thoroughbred when they see one. And while they're at it, bringing over a horsebox to steal Scottie, they reckon they might as well take Holly and her foal. The chestnut will fetch a good price. As for the little bay; any kid would fall for her the minute they set eyes on her.'

Carly and Hoody stood listening by the paddock gate. 'There's only one problem with that,' Hoody muttered.

Carly followed the direction of his gaze as he narrowed his eyes and looked across the yard. She spotted the side gate, which until now had always been locked, hanging wide open. 'You mean the thieves would've needed a key?'

He nodded and hurried across with his awkward, springy stride. 'The lock hasn't been forced,' he confirmed.

'But maybe they had some kind of master key, or some other sneaky way of opening it.' She didn't know much about burglars' methods, but she realised that often they didn't let simple locks like this stand in their way.

'Nah!' Hoody bluntly insisted he was right. 'You want to know what I think?'

'You're going to tell me anyway.' She recognised that set, stubborn expression.

'It was the Martyns.'

'Hoody, do me a favour!' He was saying that the owners had stolen their own horses! With an impatient shake of her head, she set off back across the yard to join Steve.

'Please yourself.' Hoody stayed put, slouching against the gatepost, hands in pockets, kicking with the toe of his trainer at a tuft of grass growing through a crack in the concrete.

'Hoody thinks Olivia and Kingsley Martyn did it!' Scornfully Carly reported the theory to the inspector.

'Huh.' Steve was about to dismiss the idea too. Then he thought again. 'No, wait. There could be some sense in that.'

Carly took a deep breath. Standing here discussing far-fetched theories wasn't helping them to get the horses back. They should be backtracking to the village, asking the attendant at the garage if he'd seen a horsebox driven by strangers hanging about within the last couple of hours.

'Listen!' Steve followed Hoody's hunch through. 'Say the Martyns got an early plane back because of the police message. They land late last night or early this morning with just one idea fixed in their heads.'

'Which is?'

'Which is to get rid of the evidence of their crime as fast as possible. In other words, they want to catch us off-guard, move in and take Scottie, Holly and Meg out of here to a secret location where we can't get at them. With the evidence of their neglect hidden away, our case against them collapses . . . *We need those three horses*!' Steve stressed each short word, then ended with a hollow laugh. 'Clever!'

But Carly was still doubtful. 'Why does it have to be that? If Hoody's right about it having to be someone with a key, why couldn't it be a cleaner or a gardener, who knows the Martyns are away; or a visitor!' Suddenly she had her own flash of inspiration. 'I know for a fact that a woman in a flash sports car has been hanging around Greenacres lately!'

'*How* do you know?' Steve indicated he was open

to all theories. It could be opportunist thieves. It could be the Martyns. It could even be Carly's female sports car driver.

'Miss Jennings told me about her. Then I saw her for myself!' she gabbled. This was it; a lead they could follow up straight away. A young woman with fair hair and red fingernails behaving suspiciously; she'd visited the house and realised it was empty, yet she'd come back a few days later. 'Come on, I'm going to Dower House to ask if she's been hanging around again!' she insisted, dashing headlong across the yard, almost bumping into Hoody on her way out.

'But let's not jump to conclusions,' Steve advised.

Too late: Carly already had. She was running through the open gate, across the front of the house and on to the drive, taking the quickest route down an avenue of tall, straight poplar trees to Miss Jennings' redbrick house at the end of the lane.

'Miss Jennings, please answer the door!' Carly was desperate to make her hear. She raised the lion's head knocker and rapped hard against the faded green paintwork.

'There's no one in.' Hoody stood back from the front

porch and gazed at the upstairs windows.

'I'm sure she's here!' Carly had seen the old lady as they drove by; she remembered how she'd refused to say hello and vanished inside the house. And just now, as she and Hoody ran ahead of Steve to beg for information about anything strange going on in the lane during the last couple of hours, Carly was sure that a curtain at an upstairs window had moved.

'If she's in, she doesn't want to speak to us.' Hoody stated the bald fact. 'C'mon, let's go!'

'. . . Miss Jennings!' Carly ignored him and stepped out on to the path. Unless the old lady could give them some clue, or some lead to follow, the task of finding Scottie, Holly and Meg would be like looking for a needle in a haystack. She called at the top of her voice. 'It's me, Carly! Someone's stolen the horses. We need your help!'

'Still no reply.' Like Hoody, Steve had given up hope. He began to walk, head down, towards the horsebox.

Silence from inside the house. Carly darted down the side, amongst the gnarled apple trees of an old orchard. She knocked on a side door and called again.

'Carly, let's go!' Hoody walked to the gate and held it open.

'You go. I'll come in a minute.' Unable to accept that the house was empty, she wanted to scout around the back.

'No.' Hoody stood stubbornly holding the gate.

Standing on tiptoe, she peered in through the kitchen window. There were cups and saucers on the table, a teapot and milk jug set out on a tray. She was sure that there was someone in there.

'What are you gonna do, break down the door?' Hoody asked. 'It's no good, Carly; leave it.'

A slender thread of hope broke as she nodded and stepped away from the window. He was right. But now where did they start looking for clues? The garage in Holybridge? Other neighbours? The village pub?

'The police are on their way,' Steve reported as they trudged towards the horsebox. 'They'll meet us at the Red Lion.'

Carly sighed and turned to take a last look at Dower House. 'Fine,' she murmured, her eyes prickling with tears which she tried not to show. She decided to pretend to go along with whatever plan the others made. But secretly, deep down, she had a cold, hollow feeling that they were never going to pick up the trail, and that the three beautiful horses would never be found.

'It's not like stolen jewellery or paintings; a horse is a pretty big object to steal!' Liz pointed out later that day. '*Three* horses, come to that!'

Saturday afternoon was always a busy time at Beech Hill and the appointment book was full. Liz herself had brought in a white rabbit found in a cardboard box in a phone booth outside Hillmans. The owner had felt enough of a guilty conscience to leave a plastic bag full of rabbit food in the box, and to write his name on the lid. 'Snowy' it said, in scrawly black felt-tip. A child's handwriting and a story that would never be told.

Carly had taken the rabbit out of the box and stood with him in her arms as Steve brought Liz up to speed on the case of the missing horses.

'. . . You would think!' The inspector agreed with the junior partner's point. 'It's amazing how everyone claims not to have seen a thing. The guy at the garage swears that ours was the only horsebox that passed in the last twenty four hours. The police checked all the houses for a two mile stretch along the North Wootton road; same result. Either everyone's been going around with their eyes closed, or . . .'

'They're lying!' Carly cut in. She put the rabbit on the treatment table for Liz to examine. Snowy sat hunched up and miserable, pink nose and white whiskers twitching. After five hours asking futile questions and getting no useful answers, she, Steve and Hoody had had to agree with the police sergeant that there was no point continuing to knock on doors. They'd come home tired, dispirited and empty-handed.

'Sorry,' Liz said kindly. She stroked Snowy's long, silky fur, then checked him over for cuts and bruises. 'I know how you must feel. But my advice is to keep busy and forget about the horses as much as you can.'

Steve glanced at Carly's closed-off, unhappy expression. 'Hard, I know,' he murmured. 'But Liz is right; it's time to move on. Let the police solve the crime. After all, it's what we pay them to do!'

No way! If they thought she could forget about Scottie

and the other two horses, they were crazy.

'Call someone. Go round to a friend's house,' Paul suggested when afternoon surgery was finished. He took Carly upstairs to the flat where they lived and gave her one of his 'talks'. *Things don't always work out the way you want. In this job, you mustn't take things to heart*.

Ruby lay curled in an armchair by the living-room window, catching the evening sun. Carly picked up the tortoiseshell cat without ceremony and slumped down in the chair. She stroked her hard as she endured her dad's lecture.

No one was saying what she wanted to hear. Everyone was brushing the horses off as if they didn't matter. But they were flesh and blood. They'd been dragged out of their field and shoved into a nasty horsebox. They were probably, right this minute, locked up in a dark, out of the way stable, where no one would find them. Scottie's saddle sores would need fresh ointment, Holly and Meg would be scared out of their minds.

'*Miaow!*' Ruby objected to the rough treatment. She got up from Carly's lap and stalked off.

Standing by the window which overlooked the

park, Paul pointed out Hoody and Vinny. 'Take a dog for a walk,' he suggested.

Hoody carried a stout stick. He threw it. Vinny chased and brought it back. He dropped it at Hoody's feet. The whole thing began again. 'No,' Carly sighed as her dad gave up and went to have a shower. 'I don't want to go to the park.'

'OK, Hoody, listen to this!'

'I'm listening, I'm listening!' He backed off into the football pavilion, arms raised in surrender.

Suddenly everything had changed. The evening had dragged, the night had been long and empty. But this morning Carly had had a brilliant idea. It was called lateral thinking; not following the obvious, but stepping sideways and coming at a problem from a new angle.

She'd looked up the numbers for racehorse trainers near Worcester and started to make phone calls.

'. . . Yes, sure, I know Joel Martyn,' had been the instant reply. 'A good jockey. Didn't he go and ride for Ben Shipley at Westham?'

Shipley, B, Brenton Hill Stables, Westham. Carly had gone straight to the trainer's number in the *Yellow*

Pages. Ben Shipley had said yes, sure; Joel Martyn was working for him now, and who wanted to know?

Carly had told Mr Shipley that it was about Joel's horse, Sir Walter Scott.

'Scottie?' The trainer had sounded surprised. 'I'd no idea the horse was still around. Joel never said.' He'd been willing to tell her his employee's address. 'It's a flat in the city centre,' he'd explained. 'Joel and his girlfriend just moved in last week. There's no phone connected yet.'

'28 Canalside!' Carly waved her piece of paper at Hoody. She'd written down Joel Martyn's address with care.

'What for?' Hoody tried to slow her down as he and Vinny followed her across the deserted football pitch. 'Why should I want to visit some jockey I never even heard of? Tell me that for a start!'

Canalside was a brand new development by the old manmade waterway that ran through the city. Barges still docked along the wharves, but these days they were used as houseboats or transformed into smart restaurants. The wharves were newly cobbled and lined with flowers and shrubs, and the old derelict warehouses had been pulled down to make way for lowrise blocks of flats such as Joel Martyn's new home.

'Kingsley and Olivia Martyn's son might know something about Scottie's disappearance!' Carly insisted. She led the way across a humped bridge over the grey canal.

'Says you!' Hoody wasn't hopeful. He'd listened to the story; how Joel had argued with his parents and disappeared from their lives, leaving Scottie to suffer at their hands. 'But it sounds more like he couldn't care less what happened to his horse at the time, so why should he be involved in this latest mess?'

'If we don't ask, we won't know!' Carly read the name, 'Canalside', etched into a stone slab by the main entrance to the flats. She began counting numbers along the ground floor. Ten, twelve . . . eighteen, twenty. 'That's it!' She pointed four doors along and hurried forward.

'Here, Vin!' Hoody called sharply, as the dog nosed in doorways. 'Sorry!' he mumbled to a woman who came out to shoo Vinny away from her precious potted bay tree.

By the time Hoody and Vinny had caught up with

Carly, she'd already knocked at number 28.

'Yes?' A man stuck his tousled head around the door. He was bleary-eyed and unshaven, and obviously unhappy to be disturbed.

'Joel Martyn?' Carly's confidence evaporated. She'd been so busy concocting a story that involved the son in Scottie's disappearance, that she hadn't planned what to say. And now that she stood on the doorstep, the actual theory didn't seem all that clear.

'Yes.' A pair of blue-grey eyes stared at the unexpected visitors. The door stayed closed.

Deciding not to beat about the bush, Carly stated their business. 'Your horse, Scottie, has been stolen.'

'No, you're having me on!' Joel stepped out on to the doorstep. He was medium height and build, with light brown hair cut short, dressed in a white polo shirt and tracksuit bottoms. His feet were bare. Behind him, a room full of cardboard boxes and disconnected hi-fi equipment was visible. 'What the heck would you know about my horse?'

'He was living at Greenacres.' Carly met his gaze. 'I'm from Beech Hill Rescue Centre. My dad's the chief vet there. We were called out to your parents' house because Miss . . . er, because someone in the area was worried about him and your family's two other horses.'

'*Two* other horses?' Joel backed off into his chaotic living room in bewilderment.

'Holly and her foal,' Carly confirmed.

'They bought a pregnant mare?' He let them know this was news to him.

Which meant that Miss Jennings's account had been right. Joel Martyn hadn't been near Greenacres since February. But did she really believe him? Carly studied the young jockey carefully as he stumbled backwards into a box full of books. 'All three horses were suffering from neglect,' she went on. 'Your parents went away on holiday and left them out in the field in the middle of a heatwave.'

'For God's sake!' Joel turned away and covered his eyes with his hand. He pressed his thumb and forefinger against his temples. 'I should never have left him there!'

'He's OK now.' Hoody spoke up for the first time. He was bent forward, one hand through Vinny's collar to stop the dog from sniffing around the unfamiliar room. 'Or he was until he got stolen yesterday morning.'

'And you think I know something about that?' Joel spun round and snapped back. 'You're saying I stole Scottie?'

'We're not saying anything!' Carly came between Hoody and Joel Martyn. She felt Vinny escape from her friend's grasp and brush past. 'All we're trying to do is find these three horses!'

'Why?' Joel raised his voice. He couldn't stand still any longer, but needed to stride up and down the room.

Carly was trying to decide whether or not to tell him about the cruelty case against his parents. She couldn't predict how he'd react so she sought another reason. In the pause, Vinny nosed around the hi-fi towards an open door that led into the kitchen. He reached it and padded on, sharp claws rattling against the smooth tiled floor.

'Vin!' Hoody muttered, going after him.

From her spot in the living room, Carly could see what had attracted Vinny's attention. It was pale fawn, with long, silky hair. Its ears flopped softly over appealing brown eyes. 'Golden retriever,' she whispered to Hoody.

'Vin!' he called, louder than before.

Golden retriever! Something clicked in Carly's head. *An open-topped car . . . a dog in the passenger seat.*

'Whose mongrel is this?' An irritated voice called from the kitchen. There was a scuffle of paws on tiles, a slap from a rolled-up newspaper, a surprised yelp from Vinny.

Then a figure in a dressing-gown appeared at the door: Joel Martyn's girlfriend. Carly gasped. The girlfriend had long fair hair and red fingernails. She was just the sort person to drive around country lanes in a silver sports car!

9

'Yes, I did visit Greenacres,' Elouise Edwards admitted. She sipped black coffee from a large white cup. Her fair hair, streaked blonde by the sun, fell forward across her tanned face.

'Why didn't you tell me?' Joel strode restlessly about the kitchen. 'It couldn't just have slipped your mind, could it?'

'No.' His girlfriend tossed her head and glanced away at Trudi, the golden retriever, who seemed to be getting on with Vinny like a house on fire.

'So?' Leaning on the table, Joel forced her to look at

him. 'You decide to go and see my parents without even talking it through with me. How come?'

Elouise closed her eyes. When she opened them, there were what looked to Carly like crocodile tears. 'I was only trying to help. I know that if I'd told you, you would've tried to stop me.'

'Too right!' He turned away and paced the floor again. 'You know I haven't spoken to them in months. What's more, I don't plan to go near the place until they decide to say sorry for what they did!'

'What did they do?' Carly couldn't stop the question from slipping out. She wanted to know exactly what had split the family up.

'My father made me ride Scottie in the Gold Star Handicap at Worcester, even though I told him the horse wasn't race-fit.' Joel frowned at the memory. 'And what happens? Scottie gives it everything he's got. He's in the lead, but he tires and falls at the last hurdle. He sprains a suspensory ligament; that's bad news. It means he's out of action for the rest of the season. And Dad blames me.'

Carly nodded. 'So you two had a row and you walked out?'

'Not quite.' A grim smile crossed Joel's features.

'Dad threw me out. What was worse, he said no way could I take Scottie with me. He'd shelled out the money to buy the horse, so legally he was in the right. He even threatened to have the law on me if I tried taking Scottie away.'

Hoody, who had been perched on a stool near the door, scraped it across the tiles as he stood up. He shook his head and shrugged, giving a withering look that said, 'Case proved'.

'And don't look at me as if *I'm* your horse thief!' Joel insisted. 'I swear to God I haven't been near Greenacres since the day I walked out!'

'Don't look at *me* either!' Elouise added. 'All I'm saying is that I took it on myself to try and meet with Olivia to see if between us we women could talk some sense into Joel's father. I thought the family feud had gone on long enough, that's all.'

'But you didn't manage it?' Carly prompted.

'No. I tried twice. The second time I realised that they must be on holiday and decided to postpone my mercy mission until they came back. And before you ask,' she said quickly, 'I didn't ring beforehand because I didn't want to speak to Kingsley. It was Olivia I wanted to see, remember.'

'And you did all this without saying a single thing to your boyfriend?' Hoody made it clear he didn't believe Elouise's account. 'Yeah, right!'

'OK, enough!' Joel's already brittle temper snapped. He got hold of Carly's shoulder and turned her around to face the front door. 'You come barging in here; a couple of kids and a scruffy dog. You tell me my parents are going to step off a plane and get themselves arrested . . .'

'I never . . . !' Carly began, trying to shrug him off. Vinny had jumped up and started to growl at Joel, while Hoody barged across the room, crashing into boxes as he went.

'Whatever!' The jockey was red in the face, out of control. 'You say the horse I love best in the world has nearly died from neglect, and on top of that he's been stolen!'

'I'm sorry!' Pulling herself free, Carly made it through the door.

'And then . . . !' Joel spun round to come face to face with Hoody and Vinny. 'And then you've got the nerve to accuse first me, then my girlfriend, of the theft!'

'We didn't . . . !' Carly pleaded. She stopped in mid-sentence, cut off by Joel grabbing Hoody and flinging him out of the flat. Vinny followed in a flurry of growls and barks.

'Great!' Hoody found his balance as the door slammed.

Carly gasped for breath, wandering in a semi-daze on to the cobbled wharf. How had her clever plan gone so wrong?

'They expect us to believe that!' Hoody grunted, shaking his head and giving one of his shrugs. 'Yeah, we believe it!' he yelled back at the closed door. 'Sure we do; like, we believe every single word!'

'Joel Martyn has the biggest reason to steal Scottie!' Hoody told the policeman in Reception at Beech Hill. 'He's got this massive grudge against his father. Besides, his girlfriend's been seen hanging around the area. It has to be them!'

'Thanks, Sherlock!' The policeman eyed Hoody from the tip of his beaten-up trainers to the top of his spiky hair, taking in the crumpled grey T-shirt on the way. He'd come to tell Paul Grey that Olivia and Kingsley Martyn were at that very moment on a flight back from Greece.

'At least that rules them out.' Paul's response had been the obvious one. 'They can't have stolen their own horses if they weren't even in the country at the time!'

The policeman had agreed. 'I never thought it was likely,' he'd admitted. 'It would have taken a lot of nerve to whip the evidence away from under our noses.'

That was when Hoody had piled in with the new theory about Joel and Elouise. With Steve and Liz listening quietly in the background, he'd told them how Carly's brainwave had allowed them to track down the Martyns' son. 'You should've seen him,' he insisted, pointing out a rip in the shoulder of his T-shirt where Joel had grabbed him to throw him out of the flat. 'He was way out of order.'

'And he really cared about Scottie,' Carly pointed out. 'Which makes us think that he'd be desperate to get him back.'

'But why steal Holly and Meg?' Steve pointed out the flaw in Carly and Hoody's argument. 'Surely Joel Martyn would only be interested in the thoroughbred?'

Carly frowned at Hoody. Neither had an answer to this one.

It took them back to square one. 'Which makes me think these are opportunist thieves we're talking about here.' The policeman's slow, deep comment was the voice of common sense. 'Forget the conspiracy, the family feud etcetera. Think basic. There's a spate of thefts in the area. Tack gets nicked from four or five stable yards. Eventually the villains hit on Greenacres and they can't believe their luck; three valuable horses seemingly abandoned in a field. House empty, owners away. The opportunity's too good to miss and they're back next day with a truck, ready to break the locks. Bingo!'

'So you won't even go and check up on Joel Martyn?' Hoody muttered. They'd given the policeman the Canalside address, but it looked like he wasn't going to use it.

'I didn't say I won't go and have a chat.' The policeman took his hat from the desk, nodding pleasantly at everyone. 'But it's not at the top of my list of priorities.'

'And what about the parents?' Carly asked. 'You don't think they could've called from Greece and . . .' She faltered, trying to frame a new theory. '. . . Kind of arranged to make the horses vanish?' After all, Miss

Jennings had once mentioned a girl who was supposed to water and look after Scottie, Meg and Holly. The girl had stopped calling in for some reason, but surely the Martyns could have contacted her and put her up to 'vanishing' the evidence.

'Think basic.' The policeman repeated his advice. 'Believe me, most crimes are simpler than you imagine.'

'But!' Carly murmured, as Paul showed the policeman out and Steve and Liz went into the office.

'But what?' Hoody was the only one still interested in her ideas.

'But, if they're right and we're wrong, what are the police going to do to get the horses back?'

His reply came quick and sharp. 'Nothing,' he said. 'Absolutely zilch!'

They went back to Greenacres – as if by simply going to stare at the empty field sloping away to the stream at the bottom, they could re-materialise Meg, Holly and Scottie.

But no bay foal trotted up the hill on stick-like legs, jumping and kicking for the sheer joy of it, or chasing the rabbits that squatted by burrows in the tussocky grass. And no chestnut mare drank from the clear water in the rejuvenated stream, or broke off from cropping quietly at the sweet clover to come and rub her soft nose against Hoody's palm, saying, *Where's the cavesson? Where's the lunge rein? Why aren't we working?*

There was no Scottie, head lifted proudly, his long legs and sleek roan flanks reminding you that he was no ordinary pleasure ride, but a top-class racehorse with breeding and blue blood behind his aristocratic name.

'What are we doing here?' Hoody wanted to know.

Steve and Paul had dropped them off on one of their runs to the bird sanctuary, with a warning to be careful. 'Mr and Mrs Martyn are due home any time,' Paul had reminded them. 'I don't want any confrontations. And I don't want them accusing you of trespassing, so stick to the public footpath and stay out of trouble!'

'. . . We're looking!' Carly insisted. She'd sneaked into the paddock despite her dad's advice.

'For what?'

She watched Vinny's eager nose track down a rabbit and chase it up the hill. The rabbit's white tail vanished down a hole and left the dog scrabbling in the soil at the entrance. 'Anything!' she sighed. 'A clue, a sign . . . anything!'

'Great! All I can see is grass!'

And buttercups, daisies, dandelions. Carly's gaze lifted towards the big house. Its windows were blank and empty as usual. The stable yard seemed strangely quiet, the doors bolted. But the side gate leading into the lane was swinging open.

'Hey, didn't we leave that shut last time we were here?' She quickened her pace towards the paddock gate.

'Yeah, but it could be the wind.' Refusing to get excited, Hoody followed more slowly.

'No, I think I saw someone!' A movement at least. Perhaps a figure slipping quietly away.

'You think!'

As Carly climbed the paddock gate and ran across the yard, the gate across the yard swung closed. She reached it and pushed it open again in time to see Miss Jennings hurrying out of the lane into her own back garden.

'Hey!' Without stopping to think, Carly called after the old lady. 'Hello, Miss Jennings!'

There was no reply.

'Maybe she didn't hear you.' Hoody caught her up. 'Are you sure it was her?'

'Yes!' Miss Jennings' slight, grey-haired figure and pastel clothes were unmistakeable. 'And she heard me all right.' This time, Carly was convinced that she was deliberately avoiding them. 'Come on. Let's see what she's up to!'

So they followed her quickly down the lane, only stopping at the gate which the old lady had just entered. More of a door than a gate, it led through a tall brick wall into the orchard at the back of Dower House. Hoody tried the rusty iron handle. 'Locked,' he told Carly.

'Try the front!' She ran the length of the garden, round the corner, on to the road, reaching the main gate just as Miss Jennings herself hurried through the apple trees, past the climbing yellow rose that spread over the porch at the front of her house.

'Ah!' Breathless and flustered, the old lady stopped dead. 'Carly . . . Hoody!'

'What's happened? Why are you avoiding us?' Carly pushed through the gate into the garden.

'I'm not. That's ridiculous!' She glanced behind her,

through the open door and down the hallway.

Suspicions aroused, Carly peered past her, but the hall was dark compared with the bright light of the garden. 'You are. What's wrong?'

'Nothing! You caught me by surprise. I only slipped up to Greenacres to check that the horses hadn't come back . . .' Miss Jennings' lame excuse fell flat. And she was growing more agitated, stepping back to close the front door so that Carly and Hoody couldn't see inside.

As she pulled in one direction, so someone behind the door pulled in the other. The second person was more determined.

'Wait a moment . . . oh!' The old lady let go of the door.

Out stepped a girl. She looked about seventeen or eighteen, with long, light brown hair and eyes that were between grey and blue. There was a puzzled, guarded look on her face, a readiness to step out and help Miss Jennings.

'It's all right, I'm perfectly fine!' the old lady gasped, one hand clutching the collar of her blouse.

'No, you're not.' The girl scowled at Carly, ignoring Hoody and Vinny who had stayed out on the road. A farm tractor rumbled by, its giant wheels casting off mud from the field it had just driven through. 'Do you want me to get rid of these people?' the girl yelled above the noise of the engine. She stepped forward, prepared to see Carly off the premises.

'No, really!' Miss Jennings' faint voice could hardly be heard. 'No, Claire; everything is perfectly all right!'

Carly stared back at the girl. It was the airforce-blue colour of her eyes that she locked on to. Not blue, not grey. Somewhere in between, like Joel Martyn's eyes. And the name; 'Claire'.

'You're Claire Martyn!' she whispered. The mysterious daughter. The girl away at school who'd never come home. The one who was always overlooked; poor Claire.

'There were *two* cups on the tray!' Small details clicked jerkily into place. Carly recalled Miss Jennings' kitchen table from the day before; the uneasy feeling that the old lady had been hiding from them. She pursued Claire Martyn into the house. 'You were here yesterday!'

The girl narrowed her eyes and nodded. 'What's wrong with that?'

Carly turned on Miss Jennings. 'You tell us!' she challenged. 'There must have been something wrong with it; otherwise you'd have come to the door!'

'Can't I call on my neighbour?' Stepping between Carly and the old lady, Claire was in no mood to give anything away.

'Yes, except Miss Jennings told me you hadn't been around for ages. You were supposed to be ill, then you never came home. You didn't even know about Holly and Meg!'

'That's right!' Claire's eyes flashed. 'That's ironic, isn't it? All my life I longed to have a horse and they said no. It was always "Joel needs this. Joel must have that!" Joel, Joel, Joel! In the end, I'd had enough!'

'Weren't you *ever* ill?' Carly demanded suspiciously.

'Do I look it?' The girl spread her arms wide. She was fit and tanned, as if she'd been working outside all summer. 'No, that was something my mum and dad made up to hide the fact that I'd ditched school before I took my "A" levels and gone and got a job at a riding-school!'

'Where?' Hoody dropped in his casual question.

'Never mind!' Claire took Miss Jennings' arm and led her to the kitchen where she could sit at the table and calm herself. 'It just so happens I was in the area yesterday morning and decided to call at Dower House to see Nancy.'

'What if you'd bumped into your parents?' Carly asked. 'Weren't you bothered about that?' Claire's story made sense, but there was something not right about the rushed and bad-tempered way she was telling it.

'I knew they'd be on holiday, didn't I? They always are in August.'

'And this was just yesterday?' Hoody checked. 'Not earlier in the week?'

But before they got any more answers, they heard a car speed along the North Wootton road, brake hard and turn up the lane to Greenacres. The high garden wall obscured the view from the kitchen window, but the sound of the car cut off all conversation.

'Who was that?' Claire muttered, running out the back way and flinging open the garden gate in time to see a large, dark green estate car stop at the double gates of the big house. 'Oh no!' she gasped.

'Do you know them?' Carly was next to arrive in the lane. Greenacres gates were opening by remote control, the car was easing into the drive. 'Claire?'

126

The girl's face was suddenly drained, her voice shaky. 'It's Mum and Dad!' she breathed.

10

Carly saw two figures get out of the car. The man opened the back and took out large suitcases while the woman unlocked the door. He was medium height and stocky, very tanned. She was slightly taller, slim and dressed in a bright sundress and white sandals.

'So?' Hoody said. What was all the fuss? Everyone knew the Martyns were due back to face the music.

'Do they know what happened to the horses?' Claire whispered, shrinking back into Miss Jennings' garden, taking refuge behind the high brick wall.

'No.' Carly shook her head. 'Either the police or

Steve planned to tell them when they arrived home.'

And then, as if someone had devised a crazy computer game where all the players had shown up at once to zap each other before they got zapped themselves, another car swept along the main road and slowed almost to a halt.

'Oh great!' Hoody groaned. He kept hold of Vinny's collar to stop him dashing to greet his lady friend, the golden retriever. 'Here comes your brother and his girlfriend. That's all we need!'

The silver sports car, driven by Elouise, pulled off the main road and crawled up the lane. Joel sat beside her, the peak of his cap pulled low over his forehead. From what Carly could make out, his face was grim. 'Keep going!' she heard him tell his girlfriend, as she spotted the estate car at the door of Greenacres.

'No, wait!' Claire ran back out into the lane. 'Joel, wait! It's me, Claire!'

Elouise braked hard. Joel shot forward against the dashboard, Trudi jumped up from the floor and appeared between the driver and passenger. The dog leaped out of the stationary car and ran to meet Vinny.

'Claire?' Joel got out slowly and walked towards his sister, his mouth wide with disbelief.

'So, he didn't have a clue about any of this!' Hoody admitted to Carly that he'd been wrong. 'See his face.'

'What are you doing here?' Claire asked him.

'Trying to sort out a god-awful mess that Mum and Dad have got themselves into. How about you?'

'I came to see Nancy.' Claire dropped her gaze and half turned away. 'I happened to be passing by...' Behind her, Hoody, Miss Jennings and Carly were all lined up listening to every word.

'She just happened to be passing by yesterday as well, when the horses were stolen,' Carly said in a calm, clear voice. She felt suddenly sure of herself, glancing sideways at Miss Jennings then back at Claire to see who would crack first.

It had to be either Claire or Nancy Jennings. Amidst the confused silence, Carly knew this much.

'Oh, tell them everything, Claire dear!'

Miss Jennings! Carly shot Hoody a look of triumph. Here was a woman who had probably never told a deliberate lie in her entire life. Not the best of accomplices when you decided to commit a crime.

'Ssh!' Claire batted the air with her hand. She bit her bottom lip until it turned white with the pressure.

Joel's mind worked overtime. 'Ah!' he gasped. 'I get it!'

'What?' Elouise was slower. She obviously didn't know Claire so well. 'What do you get?'

'Claire knows where Scottie is,' Carly explained. She couldn't wait for a grand confession. The door of the big house had stayed open while Kingsley Martyn unloaded the car. He came out again with his wife and they spotted the knot of people in the lane. He would be down here in a matter of minutes. 'Your sister is the one who stole the horses!'

'They're safe!' Claire Martyn promised. She said the words over and over again. Her face was wet with tears as Carly handed her a box of tissues from the shelf in Miss Jennings' kitchen. The small, old-fashioned room with its red tiled floor and oak dresser was full to overflowing. 'I took them to a place where they would be well looked after, I promise!'

'Please don't blame her!' Nancy Jennings stood up for the girl in the face, not only of Kingsley and Olivia Martyn, but of Steve Winter and Paul Grey as well. The latter had arrived to pick up Carly and Hoody, in time to stop a major row. 'All this is my fault!' she insisted. 'If I hadn't been a busybody in the first place, none of this would have happened!'

'Yes, and three horses would be dead,' Steve put in quietly. He looked sternly at Mr and Mrs Martyn. 'Let's not forget that.'

'You see, it was pure coincidence that poor Claire came along in the middle of this unhappy business.' The old lady insisted on having her say. 'I'm afraid that she did tell a white lie when she told you that it was yesterday,' she admitted to Hoody. 'In fact, the first time was on Friday, the day of the storm; her day off from work. I've always had a soft spot for Claire, you see, and she knows it. The kind-hearted girl took the trouble to call on a lonely old lady, and what did she find . . . ?' Suddenly aware of the seriousness of what she was describing, Miss Jennings faded then stopped.

'Yes, we understand.' Paul smiled kindly. 'And in a way, you thought there was nothing so very wrong with what Claire planned to do. After all, Holly had been bought as her horse, so it didn't seem exactly like stealing. The same would apply to the foal. But what about Scottie? That was harder to justify, surely.'

'Not really.' It was Claire's turn to explain. She'd dried her eyes and was able to look steadily at her parents as she spoke. 'Not when you think about the life he'd been leading here at Greenacres after Joel left. By taking him away, he was bound to have a better deal. It wasn't a hard decision to make!'

Olivia Martyn hung her head.

'Look, we didn't swan off to Greece and dump the horses without anyone to look after them!' Kingsley Martyn protested. 'It wasn't as bad as it seems!'

'How bad was it, Mr Martyn?' Steve's stern expression didn't break as he waited for the full explanation.

'We'd got in touch with Sarah Fenton and paid her to come out again and look after things. But it's obvious she didn't do that!' Kingsley Martyn refused to take the full blame, until Steve reminded him about Scottie's saddle sores, and the other infections they'd found in Holly and Meg's ears and eyes.

'A healthy horse doesn't get into that state overnight,' the inspector insisted. 'What we found was the result of weeks if not months of neglect.'

'OK, so I'm no expert,' Martyn admitted. 'I have a business to run, I'm a busy man. I left the day-to-day care to Sarah, but it's obvious she was unreliable in all directions.'

'Dad, save it, will you!' Joel stepped in angrily to stop the excuses. He ignored Elouise's restraining hand. 'Can't you for once in your life admit you got it wrong?'

'That's putting it mildly!' Hoody muttered to Carly. 'The man's family's fallen apart, three horses nearly died because of him!'

Carly jabbed him with her elbow. She was waiting to see what Mrs Martyn had to say. And most of all, she wanted Claire to own up about where she'd hidden Scottie, Holly and Meg. The small kitchen was overcrowded and hot, the looks of hate darting across the table were reaching flashpoint.

'*I* got it wrong?' Kingsley Martyn reacted angrily to his son's accusation. 'I was the one who put everything into building you a successful career as a jockey, remember!'

'Yeah, and did I ever ask you to do that?' Joel demanded. 'And what about Claire here? Your daughter, in case you forgot! I wouldn't blame her if she never told you what she'd done with the precious horses. I wouldn't if I was her!'

'Joel, don't make it any worse.' Sighing, Claire pushed her way towards the door. 'Dad's never going to change. You might as well save your breath.'

'But *I* might change.' Olivia Martyn's voice broke through the scuffle of chairs and murmurings of disappointment. 'I might be able to!'

Claire paused in the doorway, her back to her mother.

'I can try!' Olivia cried, doing her best not to break down. She pushed past her husband and followed her daughter across the room. 'If you can find it in you to forgive me, Claire, I'll do my very, very best to make up for what your dad and I have done!'

'Families!' Hoody grunted. 'It makes me glad I don't have one.'

'You've got your sister.' Carly had dragged him out to Greenacres one last time.

'Zoe doesn't count.' He was chewing a grass stalk, walking knee-deep in a field of poppies.

'Yes, she does. Anyone who washes your clothes and makes your bed counts.'

'She doesn't.' Hoody held out the hem of his one and only T-shirt. 'I wouldn't let her if she offered.'

'Anyway!' Carly couldn't be bothered to argue. The weather was too nice; breezy and bright, blue and green, with a sea of scarlet poppies.

They'd come for a special reason, a week after the showdown in Nancy Jennings' kitchen. The poppy field was next to the Martyns' paddock, the white fence just coming into view.

'Let me get this straight,' Hoody said, picking up a stick and throwing it for Vinny. 'Mrs Martyn says she's made a total foul-up of being a mother. She swears it's all gonna be different from now on?'

'You were there. You heard what she said.' To Carly it all seemed so long ago; the tears, the promises . . .

'OK, so Claire believes her. Mr Martyn doesn't come into it at this point. Claire's willing to come home and give it another go, as long as they let her bring the horses back with her. She's keeping them hidden at the place where she's gone to work; a stables near the school where she's been sent for the last six or so years?'

'Right.' Exactly that; and then it had been up to Steve and Carly's dad to agree to drop the cruelty case.

'Give them a chance,' Miss Jennings had pleaded. 'People can start afresh if you offer them the opportunity. Families can get over arguments, rifts can heal.'

'We'll drop the charges provided that Joel and Claire are given charge of the three horses,' Steve had decided. 'And provided we can call in and check them every few weeks to see how they're getting along.'

Claire and her mother had burst into tears and hugged each other. Joel had grudgingly shaken his father's hand.

'Families!' Hoody said again. He wasn't convinced.

But Carly was glad. She hoped the Martyns would be able to work things out. And she knew Joel and Claire both cared about Scottie, Holly and Meg. 'Look!' she said softly.

Joel Martyn was leading Scottie on a short lead rope towards the fence as they approached. The horse had a spring in his step, his whole body was fluid and relaxed.

'I've put him back in training,' Joel told them as they swung their legs over the fence and sat looking in on the paddock. 'The ligament's completely healed, so he'll be able to race this coming season, no problem.'

'He looks fantastic!' Carly sighed. Compared with

the horse they'd seen that day in the middle of the heatwave; that hazy, staggering, drooping wreck of a horse.

'And my dad's not putting any pressure on,' Joel assured them. 'He lets me come and go, putting in the work with Scottie whenever I want. So things are looking up!'

'Has Claire come back to stay?' Carly was disappointed that, for the moment, there was no sign of either Holly or Meg.

Joel stroked Scottie's smooth, dappled neck and grinned. 'She put one more proviso on the deal,' he told them. 'Mum and Dad had to promise not to hassle Miss Jennings. In fact, she said she wouldn't come back home unless they promised to let the old dear stay at Dower House for the rest of her life!'

'Yeah?' Hoody's eyebrows shot up, but he obviously approved. 'Cool.'

'So, did anyone thank you two yet?' Joel asked, as at last Carly caught sight of what she was looking for. Claire Martyn was leading the chestnut mare and her foal out of their stable and crossing the yard towards the paddock.

'What do you mean?' Jumping down from the